Landon Snow

and the Volucer Dragon

Landon Snow

and the Volucer Dragon

R. K. MORTENSON

BARBOUR
PUBLISHING

Other books by R. K. Mortenson

Landon Snow and the Auctor's Riddle
Landon Snow and the Shadows of Malus Quidam
Landon Snow and the Island of Arcanum

Cover and interior illustrations by Cory Godbey, Portland Studios.
www.portlandstudios.com
Cover design by Kirk DouPonce, DogEared Design, llc.
www.DogEaredDesign.com

Published by Barbour Publishing, Inc., P.O. Box 719, Uhrichsville, Ohio 44683
www.barbourbooks.com

Our mission is to publish and distribute inspirational products offering exceptional value and biblical encouragement to the masses.

ecpa Member of the
Evangelical Christian
Publishers Association

Printed in the United States of America.

Dedication

For my mom.
Thank you for inspiring me to write.

Chapter One

Landon Snow ripped another clump of grass from the earth. He'd collected two big fistfuls, his fingers clutching the soft green blades like talons. Rising from his pantherlike crouch in the shade of the willow tree, he held out his fists over the faces of his sisters, Holly and Bridget. Holly's straight, blond hair fanned out from her head, while Bridget's dark curls rippled in waves. The girls were lying on their backs dozing, blissfully unaware of the plagues about to descend on them. Grinning, Landon jiggled his fists like salt and pepper shakers, sprinkling the grass.

"Locusts! Frogs! Darkness! Blood!"

The grass fell on the girls' faces. Bridget's mouth perked in a sleepy smile. Holly's nose twitched as if she might sneeze.

"Gnats! Mosquitoes! Horseflies! Mud!"

Still sleepily smiling, Bridget raised her eyebrows and rolled over like a dog, sighing. Disappointed, Landon concentrated his remaining firepower on Holly, whose eyebrows were rearing up at each other like extremely annoyed caterpillars. Soon Holly's whole face was contorting like a restless sea. Her mouth yawed from side to side.

Landon looked at his palms. Empty except for one tiny blade. Flipping his hand back over, Landon watched the tiny blade flutter toward its mark. He held his breath. The sliver of grass was about to flit right past Holly's lips when she inhaled. Down the hatch it went, snatched from midair and vanishing like a dime down a coin slot.

Holly's face froze in midscrunch. Then she awoke.

"Ack! Blech!" Holly sat up, darting her tongue like a lizard. Crossing her eyes, she tweezed the blade of grass from the tip of her tongue and then held out her finger to look at it. She frowned. "It looks like a booger."

Landon laughed. "Now that would be gross, a plague of boogers!"

Bridget rolled back over with a snort. "What? What happened? Where am I?"

"Still at Grandma and Grandpa's," Landon said, surveying the surrounding country. They had a decent view from below the willow tree on the hill. The dappled shade from the drooping branches bounced gently with the breeze. Landon looked at his old leather Bible. The pages riffled from the wind but failed to turn. It was still open to Exodus chapter 10, where they had been reading about the ten plagues on Egypt.

"Let my people go," Landon murmured, thinking of Moses and Aaron trying to persuade Pharaoh to do just that for the enslaved Israelites.

"Button Up," said Bridget sitting. "Not Wonderwood." Her voice dragged with disappointment.

"We've been here five days already," said Holly. She looked at her wrist and gasped. "I left my watch back at the house! It's been five days and. . .and. . ." She peered up into the branches, squinting, trying to gauge the sun's location.

Landon gasped in mock horror. "Oh no! Holly! We don't know how many hours have passed today! Let alone minutes" —he stooped and lowered his voice—"or seconds, or nano-seconds, or—"

"Stop. Augh!" Holly snapped her eyes shut and covered her ears.

Landon smiled and sat down by his sisters. The truth was he was feeling as disappointed as they were. If not more. He missed his friends there, especially his truest companion, the horse named Melech.

Holly looked at Bridget. "And you've never even seen Wonderwood, Bridge. Only that strange island and the sea, and—"

"And Epops," said Bridget. "And the bears. I miss them."

From the cornfield across the fence, a rustle arose, followed by a swarm of blackbirds rising into the air and then dipping as one before rising again and flying off in a wave. Landon frowned as the trailing wisp of birds faded in the distance.

"What's wrong?" asked Bridget, eyeing him askance.

Landon stared toward the horizon, seeing only a dusky sky.

"I'm not sure," he said. "I've just got this awful feeling that something's wrong"—he blinked and turned to his sisters—"in Wonderwood."

Holly leaned closer. "Are you seeing a vision, Landon? Like the animals you saw at the football game?" Normally Holly would have whispered such questions. Landon's visions, the turning pages in his Bible, and their magical trips from the Button Up Library remained the Snow children's secrets. But out here in the open country, who could possibly hear them?

Landon closed his eyes a moment and then gazed out across the top of the cornfield. "It's like I'm not really seeing anything, except. . ."

Holly and Bridget were watching him, waiting. "Except what?" Holly asked keenly.

"Yeah," said Bridget, "what do you see?"

Landon knew the blackbirds were long gone. But he could swear he was seeing dark wisps rising from the field. Not just one but dozens of black, wavy columns rising like—

"Smoke," Landon said, nearly choking on the word. His mouth and throat had suddenly gone dry. His palms felt moist despite the cooling evening air.

Holly and Bridget looked out toward the field and shook their heads.

"Or," Landon said abruptly—his throat was tightening like a vise—"they might be *shadows*." He could barely whisper the last word.

The mysterious black clouds vanished. Landon blinked. He scanned to the left and to the right. Now he wondered if he *had* seen anything.

The children sat pensively beneath the willow.

Bridget tentatively pried the stillness. "What's it like there?"

Landon felt his mouth curl into a half smile, even as he pondered the dark foreboding that tugged at his heart. "We've told you a hundred times already, Bridge. It's a forest of huge trees, with especially huge Whump Trees that people could live inside. And then there's Ludo's tree, the biggest of them all, which looks like—"

"Twenty-seven," Holly interrupted.

Landon arched his eyebrows. "What?"

"We've told her what it's like *twenty-seven* times. Not 'a hundred.' Unless you've told her another seventy-three times when I wasn't there."

Landon stared at her. "You're kidding, right? You've seriously counted the times I've told Bridget about Wonderwood?"

Holly smugly shrugged.

"I want to hear about it," Bridget said quietly. "In case, well, in case we don't get to go there this time."

Landon lay on his back and clasped his fingers behind his head, gazing up at the willow's canopy. Holly and Bridget did the same so that their elbows nearly touched to form a triangle.

The great thing about a summer day in northern Minnesota is that it never wants to end. Daytime clings to rays of sunlight, stretching them like a child refusing to relinquish a favorite blanket. Even when the sun dips past the horizon, the sky resists giving in to darkness. Landon loved this time of day, a perpetual dusk.

"It started when I got the dream-stone and Bartholomew G. Benneford's old Bible for my birthday almost two years ago." He turned to glance at the ancient book lying nearby.

As Landon continued recounting the tale of his climbing the

Book of Meanings and meeting Melech as a giant chess knight and following the clues to solve the Auctor's Riddle, it dawned on him that he was turning into a storyteller like his Grandpa Karl. This thought pleased him, warming him inside.

"You're next, Holly," Landon said some time later.

"Really? I get to tell about the shadows of Malus Quidam this time?"

At the mention of the strange, evil name, a subdued mood settled over them. Landon thought again of the flock of blackbirds and of his vision of smoke or shadows. Holly brightened the mood with the mention of the fireflies lighting up the gold dome like "fireworks flying around." With no dim corner to escape to, Malus Quidam had been defeated. Temporarily.

Finally, it was Bridget's turn to talk about her one adventure, not to Wonderwood, where the previous two had occurred, but out to sea and then to the Island of Arcanum. When she finished, remembering their sudden return from the ship's storeroom to Grandma Alice's kitchen pantry, Landon felt his stomach rumble.

"Hungry," he said.

"Me, too," said Holly in response. "I could use a bedtime snack."

"Is it really that late?" said Landon. A faint pink ribbon was warding off the blanket of deep purple pushing across the sky.

"Yeah, even without my watch, I'm pretty sure it is."

Bridget sprawled and yawned, tapping her brother and sister with her outstretched hands.

"But remember," said Landon, "these stories are just for us.

We don't tell them to anyone else. Right, Bridget?" He swiveled his head her way.

"I know. I know. I won't tell anyone."

Landon turned his head the other way. "Right, Holly?"

Holly sighed. "For the twenty-eighth time, yes. Secret. Of course."

"All right," Landon said, confident in the willow's ability to keep their shared secret.

Landon stood with his Bible and helped his sisters up. As they started down the hill toward their grandparents' house, a voice caught them from behind.

"Right, right, right. Go. It's about time you get off my property."

Landon and his sisters came to a dead halt and then turned around. Landon could see no one on or around the hill. Reluctant to move, he decided to at least put on a brave front for Holly and Bridget.

"Who said that?" He forced himself to speak louder than he wanted. When no response came, Landon grudgingly climbed the hill. "Who said that?" he practically yelled at the field of corn. He felt bolder from his place beneath the willow.

A slight movement caught Landon's eye. A figure was propping himself on the top rail of the fence. He was difficult to see. Based on the stranger's voice, Landon guessed it was a boy a little older than himself. The boy leaned from the other side of the fence, rows of corn spread behind him.

"I did. Whatcha gonna do about it?" The movement Landon had noticed was a wavering piece of straw sticking out from the boy's mouth. It waggled even more when he spoke.

Holly and Bridget came alongside their big brother. Landon wanted to get a closer look at the stranger, but he wasn't quite ready to actually approach the fence.

"This isn't your property," Holly scoffed, and Landon touched her on the shoulder to be careful.

"Yeah," said Bridget, "it's ours."

Landon grabbed Bridget's arm. "It's not *ours*," he said loudly, "but it is our grandparents', and we're staying with them." Why did he add that last part? Oh well, it was probably fairly obvious anyway.

The boy made a crude snorting sound and spat on the ground on Landon's side of the fence.

"Should have been *my* grandfather's land—and my *great*-grandfather's land," said the boy. "And my *great-great*-grandfather's. And my great-great-*great*-grandfather's land." The boy's voice grew louder with each generation. "But that's okay!" he announced. "Because one day, it's all going to be mine."

"Come on," Landon said decisively, pulling at Bridget and then tapping Holly. "Let's go. We don't need to talk to him."

"And you clean up that spit!" Bridget shouted over her shoulder. Landon yanked her forward even as he smiled at her daring. Where did his sisters find their nerve? There was a fine line sometimes between bravery and foolishness, especially when you didn't know with whom, exactly, you were dealing.

They'd gone about ten paces when a thought struck Landon. It grabbed his pounding heart and squeezed it tight. How long had the boy been standing there? More importantly, how much had he *heard*?

Suddenly, Landon felt as if he were moving in slow motion. Windows in Grandma and Grandpa Snow's house were glowing. The barn behind their house was lit, too. Grandpa must be working on his jalopy, his never-ending project. Landon was tempted to turn around and ask the boy what he'd heard. At the very least, he wanted to know if he had heard about all their adventures.

"Hey!"

Landon nearly jumped at the boy's shrill voice. When he turned, the boy was standing on the hill under the willow tree.

Landon tucked the Bible beneath his arm and clenched his fists, anger overtaking his worry.

"You say you saw smoke?" the boy mocked. "I don't see any smoke from up here."

Oh no, Landon thought. The stranger had heard *everything*.

"I'll tell you one thing, though," the boy stated loudly. "If there is smoke, then there's sure to be a fire!"

With that, the figure dipped behind the hill, laughing wickedly.

Chapter Two

Landon stared at the darkening hill beneath the drooping willow, his heart dropping. The boy had heard everything. Everything.

Their secret was out. What should he do?

Not much I can do about anything now, Landon thought. It was too late, and it was getting dark.

With one last glance over his shoulder—*he could be spying on us right now, and we couldn't see him*—Landon sighed and trudged onward. "Come on," he said sadly. "Let's go." Heartening him a little was the sight of the growing light in his grandparents' windows.

As Holly and Bridget marched on either side, Landon slowly swung his Bible like a pendulum. With each upswing, the thick book's momentum pulled him forward. Soon Bridget began mimicking her brother's lurching step. Then Holly joined in.

Landon propelled himself faster, and then he tucked the Bible like a football and began to jog. When Holly and Bridget rushed ahead, Landon shifted to a higher gear and sprinted past them, all the way to the house. His sisters arrived panting, and they all waited outside to catch their breath. It seemed all three of them had needed to burn off some energy after their encounter with the eavesdropping boy.

"What do we tell Grandma and Grandpa?" said Holly as her breathing slowed.

"Well, we still don't tell them what we were talking about," said Landon. "But I'm going to ask them who he is. He must be a neighbor."

"He was mean," said Bridget. "I bet he didn't even clean up his spit."

Landon snorted, though he still kind of ached about the whole thing inside. "No, I'll bet he didn't, either. Though we can hope he stepped on Holly's booger, at least."

"Wha—" Holly frowned, and then her face relaxed. "Oh," she said. "Yeah."

Landon and his sisters went inside to find Grandpa Karl reading in his brown leather easy chair by the fireplace. Grandma Alice was working in the kitchen. Her voice rang out before she even saw them.

"They've returned! And just in time for brownies." She turned from the oven and smiled. "Why don't you three wash up and join your grandfather and me at the table?"

The grandfather clock beneath the upstairs landing began to chime. Each deep *bong* nearly faded before the next one struck.

The sounds were soothing in some strange way, and they seemed so—*bonnnnnnggggggg*—so. . .*patient*. Landon waited for the final chime to sound before turning on the faucet. Ten o'clock. It was late.

Grandpa Karl eyed the three children as they filed into the dining room without saying a word. Finally, with what Landon thought was a look of suspicion or at least sharp curiosity, Grandpa Karl said, "You were out there quite some time."

"We didn't go to the library," said Landon, garnering funny looks from both his sisters. "Um, I mean, we were just sitting on the hill. Talking. And stuff."

Landon's face burned. Why had he said that? The *library*? He decided to stuff a brownie into his mouth before he said anything else he didn't intend to.

"Actually, I fell asleep, Grandpa," said Bridget.

"And so did I," blurted Holly. "After I'd counted the clouds."

Landon looked at Holly and frowned. "The cloudth?" he said through a mouthful of brownie. "What—"

Holly frowned back and then smiled sweetly at her grandparents. "I counted all of them before I fell asleep."

"Oh?" said Grandma Alice. "And how many were there, Holly?"

"Zero."

"Ah," replied Grandma Alice, though she didn't look very amused. Maybe she was tired. Or. . .

"I was starting to get a little worried about you," she said. The bite of brownie Landon swallowed suddenly lost some of its flavor. The gulp also carried down some guilt. Grandma Alice could make them feel guilty with her eyes.

"Yeah," said Grandpa Karl, gazing at a picture on the wall behind the children's heads, "your grandmother almost sent out a search party for you."

"A party?" said Holly.

Grandpa Karl looked at her. "Yeah. A party of one." He smiled wryly. "Me and my"—he shifted his gaze at Landon—"flashlight."

Landon gulped a piece of brownie down almost whole, which made his eyes water. Blinking, Landon grabbed his glass of milk and drank it noisily, lifting his chin toward the ceiling. "Ahh!" He set the glass back down. "That was good. Thanks, Grandma." He tried to sound cheerful.

Grandma Alice's lips smiled, but her eyes didn't. Landon had to look at the table. The evening had started out so great, but now things just kept on getting worse. Feeling miserable, Landon thought maybe the best thing he could do was go to bed and hope that everything would be better in the morning. He started to get up, then he remembered the mysterious boy by the fence. Landon knew he wouldn't be able to sleep without asking about him. With a sigh, Landon sat back down.

Grandpa Karl had that curious glint in his eye. "Something troubling you, Landon?"

Landon couldn't help nodding. He looked at his sisters. They appeared about as miserable as he was. At least mentioning the boy might distract Grandma Alice from her displeasure over their late return home. Maybe.

"There was some kid out there," said Landon finally. "A boy

on the other side of the fence."

Grandma Alice glanced at Grandpa Karl, though he kept his eyes settled on Landon. Landon thought he caught a slight twitch at the corner of one of his grandfather's eyes. Grandpa Karl's jaw slid sideways a notch as he appeared to be pondering something. "Must be the Westmoreland boy," he stated finally.

"Well, of course it must be!" Grandma Alice exclaimed, causing Landon and his sisters to sit up straight in their seats. Grandpa Karl remained still, other than his working jaw muscles.

"That boy," Grandma Alice said raising her hands. She was suddenly more animated than usual, especially at such a late hour in the day. "He's been snooping around here before. And he doesn't even live next door."

That answered Landon's next question. So he moved on to another one.

"Where does he live?"

To which Holly added: "Why does he come over here? What's his problem, anyway?" Holly's annoyance carried clearly in her voice.

Grandma Alice's eyes were wide. Her hands had moved down to the table, though her fingers were playing it like a piano. She seemed to be trying to control herself. "He's up to no good, that's all I know. I really don't trust those people. I know we ought to love and respect everyone. And I try—I really do. But those Westmorelands. . ."

Grandpa Karl slid his hand over to one of Grandma Alice's hands and covered it. She closed her eyes at his touch, though her eyeballs appeared to rove restlessly behind their lids. Landon was almost breathless as he watched her. Grandma Alice had never behaved like this, at least not in front of him and his sisters.

"It's a long story," said Grandpa Karl as he studied his grandchildren. He seemed to be debating whether to tell them more, and Landon silently willed his grandfather to share the story. "We're old enough to handle it," he wanted to say. "Come on, Grandpa. Please tell us."

Landon's prayer was answered.

"It runs deep," said Grandpa Karl. "All the way back to the founders of Button Up. Yes," he added, as if reading Landon's thoughts, "to the time of Bartholomew G. Benneford himself."

Grandpa Karl went on to say that the Westmorelands used to be the Westmorelandfields, and before that they were known as the Westmorelandfieldshire family. To everyone else in Button Up, they were quietly referred to as the *Want*moreland people, because that described their greedy hearts.

"Percy *Want*morelandfieldshire settled on the east side of Lake Button Hole about the time Bartholomew G. Benneford had built his first cabin on the western side."

"That's the Reading Room by the library lobby now, right?" asked Bridget.

"Yes," said Grandpa Karl, warming up at telling the story, even if it involved people he didn't like. "Bart's Reading Room is the only remnant of his original cabins. Thank goodness they attached it to the library when they did." He nodded to himself.

"Well, once Bart had built his House of Knowledge and Adventure, which was still farther west and which has become the cornerstone of sorts for the community, young Percy tried to purchase the rest of Bart's cabins along the lake. But Bart refused."

"How come?" asked Holly. As money was all about numbers, she had a rather keen interest in finances. "Didn't Percy offer enough?"

"That wasn't it," replied Grandpa Karl, "so much as what he wanted to do with the land."

"What did he want to do?" said Landon.

Grandpa Karl's eyebrows jumped and then fell. "Nothing," he said flatly. "He only wanted to own it, just to own it. Whereas the people who did purchase the cabins turned some of them into a resort, and they opened the rest of the property up to the public. Today it's the Lake Button Hole Park. Still privately owned and still publicly appreciated."

Grandpa Karl went on to describe that ever since Bart's refusal to sell property to Percy, the Westmoreland(fieldshire)s had carried a grudge against the entire town of Button Up, right on down through the generations. The Westmorelands owned the same parcel of land on the east shore of the lake that Percy had originally settled. Some had moved away over the years, of course, as the family had grown. But it hadn't grown that much. At least two of Percy's descendants had gone to jail for robbery.

"Armed robbery," said Grandma Alice sadly. "Too much greed."

"I hate to categorize people," said Grandpa Karl. "But they have been a hard, bitter, lonely lot." He inhaled deeply and sighed. "There's just the one boy now. One son to the current homesteaders. Maximillian."

Landon had become so enthralled by the story that he'd nearly forgotten the boy they'd seen out by the hill.

"Maximillian?" said Landon. "That's his name?"

"What a name," said Holly sarcastically. "*Maxi* and *million*. They do sound greedy."

Grandma Alice smiled for the first time all evening.

"Maximillian Westmorelandfieldshire," said Grandpa Karl. "Or Max Westmoreland for short."

"Max is a meanie," said Bridget before gaping her mouth to let out a yawn.

"It is sad to talk about Max and his entire family like this," said Grandpa Karl. "If you meet him again, just try to be kind. We'll keep loving them from afar and praying for them."

Grandpa Karl grew quiet. Eventually the *tick-tock* from the hallway drifted into the room. Landon was beginning to feel more sorry for Max than angry at him, though it still bothered him that Max had overheard them talking about the secret passageway to the library and their adventures in another land. Maybe—hopefully—Max thought they were just making the stories up. Or that they had read about them in a book somewhere and were pretending that *they* were the characters who had experienced them. Well, thought Landon, there wasn't much he could do about it now.

Pushing his chair back from the table, Landon stood. His sisters followed his cue and did the same. Before saying goodnight and retreating to Grandpa Karl's study, Landon thought of another question.

"Why does he come over here to your house? The lake is

almost a mile away."

Grandpa Karl licked his lips before answering. "Well," he said, "I think it may be that we're on the way."

" 'On the way'?" asked Landon. "On the way where?"

"To the BUL," said Grandpa Karl. "The Button Up Library." The old man's eyes stared intently at Landon through his spectacles. "Young Max has been caught trying to break into Bart's place recently. More than once."

"Yes," said Grandma Alice, shaking her head. "From what I've heard, the boy doesn't even care to read. So isn't that the strangest thing? What on earth would he want to do in the library? And so late at night?"

Landon sensed Holly and Bridget were looking at him. For some reason, he found he couldn't look away from his grandfather just yet. At least not until Grandpa Karl said, "Yes, it's very strange. Very strange behavior indeed."

After Landon said his goodnights and thanked Grandma Alice again for the brownies, he padded thoughtfully down the hall to the study. There was something in Grandpa Karl's look when he'd said, "Very strange behavior indeed"—something of a twinkle or a twitch. When Landon entered the study, he heard the grandfather clock begin to chime a leisurely count to eleven. The Bible, which Landon was sure had been closed when he had set it on the desk earlier, was lying open to Exodus chapter 3, which Landon and his sisters had read that morning. Switching on the lamp, Landon leaned closer. Some of the words were underlined but not by pencil or quilled ink. These lines were green and faintly fuzzy—as if thin blades of grass had been pressed perfectly beneath the sentences.

After quietly closing the door to his grandfather's study, Landon began to read the underlined words:

> *And the angel of the Lord appeared unto him in a flame of fire out of the midst of a bush: and he looked, and, behold, the bush burned with fire, and the bush was not consumed.*

Down a few paragraphs stretched more green lines:

> *And the Lord said, I have surely seen the affliction of my people which are in Egypt, and have heard their cry by reason of their taskmasters; for I know their sorrows.*

As soon as Landon had read the word *sorrows*, the page turned on its own. Landon gulped and then studied the next page:

> *Come now therefore, and I will send thee unto Pharaoh, that thou mayest bring forth my people the children of Israel out of Egypt.*

An ominous feeling crept over Landon, although he didn't understand why. God called to Moses from a burning bush and told him to go to Pharaoh and to lead the children of Israel— who were slaves in Egypt—to freedom. It was the beginning of the story of the Exodus, the event for which the book was named. *Exodus* meant "way out, exit, escape."

Landon closed his eyes. Why were these words underlined? What was he supposed to get from this? When he opened his eyes, another word on the page caught his attention. The word was underlined in green but was easy to miss because it was just one word and it was a small word at that. The word was *Go*. Something compelled Landon to speak it aloud—"Go"—and just like that, the bookcase behind him began to slowly swing out from the wall.

Chapter Three

Landon turned to face the opening in the wall behind the
bookcase in his grandfather's study. The word from the Bible,
Go, seemed to be echoing inside his mind. Landon took one
step toward the black doorway, but then he hesitated. Though
he'd been yearning for another adventure and a trip back to
Wonderwood—or to the sea as the case may be—he suddenly felt
unprepared and a little scared. "I'm not ready," Landon said to
the doorway and to the room and to the One he sensed was also
present in the room.

Go.

"I need my flashlight."

The flashlight was standing upright on the floor near the
couch, covered by Landon's sleeping bag. Landon picked up the
flashlight.

Go.

"I need some help," said Landon. "Can my sisters go, too?"

Nothing happened. Landon held his breath. Then he heard the sound of pages fluttering on the desk. He turned around to find this passage—again mysteriously underlined in green—in Numbers chapter 11:

And I will come down and talk with thee there: and I will take of the spirit which is upon thee, and will put it upon them; and they shall bear the burden of the people with thee, that thou bear it not thyself alone.

Landon took that as a yes. "Thanks," he said, and he quickly left the study.

Holly and Bridget were staying in the same room upstairs. Landon sidestepped the one creaky step near the top of the staircase and crept to their door. Thankfully, their parents weren't in the other upstairs bedroom, so he needn't worry about waking them. They were off on an adventure of their own, sailing on a cruise ship to Alaska. Landon gave the door five raps, waited a moment, and then eased it open.

"Holly! Bridget!" he whispered urgently.

Holly was sitting up in bed playing on her calculator. Surprisingly, Bridget was also still awake. She rolled over and looked at him. "Hi," said Bridget.

"What's going on?" said Holly. She turned her attention back to her calculator, pressed it twice, and then set it on her lap.

"It's time to go," said Landon. His heart was beating from excitement and from something akin to dread. Excitement mostly. Something strange was going on.

"I just got into bed," said Bridget, although without much complaining in her voice.

"How do you know?" said Holly, who already had her feet on the floor. "Did the pages turn?"

Landon nodded.

"On their own?" She raised her eyebrows.

Landon nodded again. "Yes. And the words were underlined in green."

Bridget made a face.

Holly said, "Green? Like a highlighter?"

"No," said Landon. "Like from grass pressed onto the pages."

Holly's eyebrows fell and her shoulders sagged. "Oh, Landon. And I suppose the pages were in the book of Exodus, too."

Now Landon raised his eyebrows. "Yeah," he said. "How did you know that?"

Holly rolled her eyes. "That's where the Bible was open, and you were throwing grass all over the place." She sighed. "Duh."

Landon clicked his flashlight on and off. Holly's eyes momentarily widened. "You didn't see shadows, too, did you?" She lifted her feet from the floor and glanced downward, scanning the floorboards for creeping blotches of darkness. This time she wasn't mocking him.

"No," said Landon. "No shadows. At least not that I saw. But the bookcase is open. . . ."

Bridget slowly sat up, glancing back and forth between her big sister and big brother. "Really?" said Bridget. "Grandpa's bookcase is really open?"

Landon could feel the air being sucked out of the room as his sisters both inhaled and held their breath.

"And it's the strangest thing," he said somberly, "but I have a feeling something's wrong in Wonderwood. Like our friends might be in trouble." He restlessly thumbed the flashlight switch, clicking it on and off several times.

"The animals, too?" Bridget asked in a high voice.

"Everybody," Landon said. *Click, click.*

Holly stood up. "We'll get dressed and be down in a minute. Come on, Bridget. There's a mission at hand."

Landon closed the door and stepped carefully down the stairs. The rhythmic *tick-tock* of the grandfather clock picked and plucked bits of silence from the air. When Landon reached the bottom, he turned down the hallway toward the study, and then he paused. Maximillian Westmoreland had heard them talking about the bookcase opening in the middle of the night and the secret passageway leading to the library. The library that Max had been trying to break into late at night recently. He'd also been spotted nosing about Grandma Alice and Grandpa Karl's property. Landon's heart froze. How long had he been away from the open bookcase? Only a few minutes, but. . .

Landon pivoted and strode to the front door. It was secure. He half sighed with relief, saving the other half until he returned to the study and checked the window. It, too, was shut and locked. Okay, he thought, smiling to himself. Just a little flash of paranoia there.

In the doorway atop the secret set of stairs, the air felt only slightly cooler than it did throughout the house. Not much of a draft and not too musty. Landon was shining his flashlight down the stone steps when he heard footsteps behind him. He turned and flashed the beam across his sisters' pale faces. He'd never seen Bridget's eyes so wide and unblinking. Holly's mouth was agape. Landon snorted a little laugh. It was good to have his sisters with him. Whatever lay ahead of them, at least they would be together.

Go.

With a wave of the light that meant, "Follow me," Landon started down the steps. "Ready or not," he whispered to the darkness ahead of him, "here we come."

Holly counted her steps down the stairs, through the tunnel, and up the stairs at the other end. Landon hardly noticed, however, as he led the way while Holly brought up the rear with Bridget between them. Every now and then, Bridget would make a little sound or utter a little word. "Oh. . .mm. . .my. . .huh."

Landon kept thinking of Maximillian and the open bookcase behind them. What if the boy did sneak into the house and follow them down here? Landon smiled at the thought of the mean kid getting trapped inside the tunnel between the two closed bookcases. Like the Egyptian army being caught by the waves of the Red Sea after following the Israelites into it. Landon immediately regretted this thought and felt guilty about it. Being trapped underground would be a horrible experience, even for a mean kid.

When Landon reached the top of the far stone staircase and touched the backside of the bookcase in Bart's Reading Room, he was vaguely aware of Holly repeating her last counted number over and over again. She was only four steps behind him, but

Landon knew she wouldn't count those final four steps until she put her foot on them herself.

This was Bridget's first time down the tunnel. "Where are we?" she whispered nervously. "What's that? Is it locked?"

Holly murmured, "Four hundred twenty-five, 425, 425."

"Nothing," Landon said, trying to concentrate. Now what would be the magic password to open the bookcase this time? On his previous two trips from the study to the library, a phrase he'd read from the Bible had done the trick. Holly's number was invading his head. Exodus, he thought. What was the chapter and verse? Exodus 425, 425, 425.

Landon almost shouted, but he bit his tongue. Forget the numbers, he told himself. Just remember the *words*. It's always the words that count. Count. Count. Count the numbers, 425. . .

No! Landon shook his head. It's the words that *matter*. What were the words? Squeezing his eyes shut to concentrate, all that Landon could come up with was one word. One little word. One little word that was underlined in green.

"Go," said Landon. "Go!"

The bookcase seemed to have heard him. The wall of wood began moving away. Landon took Bridget's hand and pulled her through the dark doorway.

"Four hundred twenty-six, 427, 428, 429." Holly stopped. Tapping Landon's shoulder, she said, "We're in."

"Yeah," said Landon shining the flashlight around the room. "We're definitely in, but in *where*?"

The bookcase closed behind them with a gentle creak, and Landon turned his light on it. No wonder it had opened so easily this time—the bookcase was empty.

Stacks of crates cluttered the room. In the middle, where Bart's reading chair should be, stood a large barrel. Landon shone the light on it. It was a very old-looking barrel, unlike anything Landon had ever seen. Except the strange thing was that it didn't really look *old*. The wood looked rough but new. And two brass hoops gleamed to a polished shine. Landon sniffed. Woodsy. Fresh. And—he directed the beam toward the stone fireplace—sooty. Yes, someone had recently burned a log or two in the fireplace!

Something was very odd about all this.

"It *looks* like Bart's Reading Room," Landon admitted. "But it looks totally different at the same time."

"No fish," said Bridget pointing above the mantel.

"And no books." Landon flashed the light at the bookcase.

"And what's up with these crates?" added Holly.

A birdcall came from outside. The children turned and stared at one another. Soon a chorus of birds was chirping and singing right outside the library. Wasn't it still the middle of the night?

As if to answer this question, faint light began to filter through slits and cracks in the walls. And through a streaky window.

"But this is impossible," Landon muttered mostly to himself. "There's not a window in Bart's Reading Room. Is there?"

"And the light," added Holly, "is coming in from everywhere." She pointed to the door that led to the library lobby. "Even from that wall. Look!"

She was right. The gradually growing light—which had to be morning sunlight—appeared between some of the stacked logs of the wall and from under the door.

Landon stared back at the mysterious window. "I've got a funny feeling. . . ." His voice trailed off as he strode toward it. "Oh my goodness. Look at this."

His sisters joined him and peered outside. Trees. Lots of trees. Beyond the trees, the world appeared to twinkle and sparkle. When he heard ducks quacking followed by what he thought was a distant splash, Landon felt a chill run down his spine.

"We're not at the Button Up Library," he stated.

"What do you mean?" said Holly. "This is Bart's—"

"Cabin," said Landon. "Yes. But it's not attached to the library. It's not Bart's Reading Room. At least not yet."

"What's going on?" asked Bridget.

Landon looked at Holly, and then at Bridget, and then around the room that suddenly didn't appear so old anymore. No wonder it smelled so woodsy and fresh. "This is Bart's first cabin, the one they moved from Lake Button Hole"—he gestured out the window with his thumb—"to the corner of the library once the rest of the library was finished."

"You mean—" Holly started.

"Yes," said Landon. "The cabin is back by the lake, where it was first built."

"But how?" Bridget piped up.

Landon waved his hand. "The cabin hasn't moved," he said. "We have. It seems we've somehow gone *back in time* and come up in the cabin *before* it was moved to the library."

Holly stated, "If that's true, that means Bartholomew G. Benneford is still alive."

The chill Landon had felt earlier now became an electric buzz throughout his body. *Old Bart's still alive!* Landon gathered his wits about him and decided to step outside to investigate. Before he reached the cabin door, however, a *thump* came from the fireplace, followed by a voice crying, "Ow!"

Chapter Four

In the fireplace sat a boy covered head to toe in black, sooty ash. Only his eyes appeared white until he opened his mouth to reveal his teeth. The boy pointed toward the empty bookcase along the wall. "So that's your secret passageway, huh? And it goes to your grandparents' house?"

Landon recognized the boy's voice, if not his shadowy form. "You!" he said accusingly. "How did *you* get in here?"

The boy almost stood, which would have knocked him against the stone mantel. Unfortunately, he caught himself in time and lowered back down to a crouching position. He gestured toward himself. "How does it look like I got in, genius?" He licked his lips and then spat. His mouth glowed along with his eyes. "I didn't think they used this fireplace anymore. Last time I climbed through, it was clean. Blech."

"Blech to you—you. . .you *spitter*!" Bridget was still upset over the boy's discharge of saliva over the fence.

Landon checked Bridget's advance toward the fireplace with a hand on her shoulder. Max's startling appearance had caused Landon to momentarily forget where they were—in the cabin by the lake back in time and not in the reading room attached to the library.

"Heave!" A man shouted from outside. Suddenly the whole cabin lurched, causing crates and children alike to lean or skid in the direction of the window. Then the floor leveled off. Landon took a step and braced himself against the barrel in the cabin's center, which hadn't budged. Whatever was inside, it must be heavy. Landon thought he heard a faint sloshing sound from within.

"Steady!" Another man's voice came from outside. "That's it. A little higher. Stop!"

The cabin swung very gently like a ship on a calm sea. It also seemed to be turning. The relative stillness was short-lived.

"Move the wagon under it. More. . .more. . .there!"

Were those horses marching beneath them?

"Drop the cabin!"

Oh no!

Like a giant elevator cut loose, the cabin suddenly fell. *Crash!* Landon picked himself up off the floor, grateful he hadn't smashed his head against the barrel. Glancing around, he saw Holly and Bridget had also fallen down but were not hurt. Max was still inside the fireplace. A fresh heap of ash had dumped on him from the chimney. As Max choked and sputtered amid a cloud of dust, Landon stifled a giggle.

Something thudded on the roof, and then a rope lashed against the window. The men outside were tying the cabin down. *They're securing it to a wagon*, Landon thought. With a curious thrill, it dawned on him that the men outside were about to move the cabin up to the library—with the children inside!

"Hyah! Hyah!" The snapping of reins was followed by a lurch, and then they were moving steadily, if bouncingly and rockingly, along the ground. The others appeared too stunned to speak. Landon was a bit tongue-tied at the moment, too.

Using the barrel for balance, he climbed to a standing position. Carefully finding his footing, he moved to the window and grasped the thin ledge protruding beneath it. Trees passed by outside. Landon held on tighter as they ascended a slope and the trees gave way to fields and prairie around them. After several minutes, Landon spotted something across the tall grass. Leaning closer to the window, he stared until he was sure of what he was looking at.

"Our hill," he said. The creaking wood and squeaking wagon wheels and *clip-clop* of hooves covered his voice. "Holly! Bridget! Look! Our hill!"

The girls clambered over and held on beside him. "Are you sure?" asked Holly.

The tree atop the hill was very small. But something told Landon it was their friendly willow.

"That's it," said Landon. "And there—that's where Grandma and Grandpa's house will be in a few years." Boy, did it feel weird saying *that*. "I wonder when their house was built," he muttered. The Button Up Library, he thought, had been completed in the early 1860s.

A foul breath drifted to Landon's nostrils.

"About 1900," said Max. Not only was he filthy with soot, but he smelled as if he hadn't brushed his teeth in a while. He had snuck up on them by the window.

"Oh!" Holly grimaced. "Don't touch me!" Her expression softened. "How do you know when our grandparents' house was built?"

Max grinned mischievously. The visual evidence of his teeth up close matched the foulness of his breath. "I know about all the properties in Button Up County: when each building was built, when ones were burned down—I mean when some of them *happened* to burn down." His grin broadened nastily. "When some were rebuilt. Who owns the deeds to what. Everything."

Holly turned her attention to the outside scene. A spider had begun crawling out upon its web in the corner of the window. "Sounds boring," said Holly.

Landon sensed the tension among them with Max's unwelcome presence. Still, he couldn't help feeling some admiration for Max's acquired knowledge of the town. He decided to test him.

"So what year are we in, then?" he said. "Supposing they're taking us up to the library to complete it right now?"

Max's grin remained, while an eerie gleam shone from deep within his eyes. "Yes," he said solemnly, "this is the year for the

House of Knowledge and Adventure: 1861."

For some reason, Landon wished he hadn't asked. Max's look and tone seemed somewhat ominous. Dangerous, in fact—though Landon was unsure why. He frowned at the dirty boy and then looked out the window.

They had reached the edge of where Grandma and Grandpa Snow's property would be and were descending the hill. *We're almost there.* Landon's misgiving about Max turned to excitement about the library. He couldn't believe they were actually going to be here for the moment of its completion. *We're making history,* Landon thought.

"I know a few things about the history of Button Up, myself," Landon said as they reached the bottom of the hill. "At least about this library and its founder," he added.

"*We* know a lot, too," said Bridget. "Our grandpa tells us lots of stories."

Max snorted. "Your grandfather and his stories." He scowled. "And as for the *founder* of this place, Bartholomew G. Benneford, for all I care, he and his precious library can go to—"

"Hey!" Before he could stop himself, Landon took hold of Max's arm and thrust him away from the window.

Max staggered back, sneering. "All the problems in this town started with your great-great-*great*-grandfather and old Bart the Fart Benne—"

Landon lunged at Max and shoved him in the chest.

Max's white-rimmed eyes flared. "You'll be sorry you did that, Landon Snow." His tone conveyed his conviction, yet Landon would not back down.

"You don't talk about our relative *or* Bartholomew G. Benneford that way," said Landon. His own tone, unfortunately, carried only a nervous tremor. He was practically trembling with rage.

"Yeah." Holly stepped alongside her brother.

Bridget spat dryly at the floor, leaving no mark. "Yeah!" she added her support to her siblings.

Landon didn't know whether to be grateful for their boldness or embarrassed by their bluntness.

"Bridget," Landon said softly. "Don't spit. Don't stoop to *his* level."

"I'm not!" she protested. She tried to spit again. "I've got a fly in my mouth. Pah-*tooey*! Yuck. There."

"Well," said Max sniggering, "you know where flies like to land."

Landon was seething, though he kept himself in check. He had never before met a person on earth who could bring out such. . .such loathing in him. He hated the feeling, but there it was. His grandmother was right: Max Westmoreland was a despicable human being.

"You're wrong, anyway." Landon was staring down Max. "My great-great-great-grandfather—*our* grandfather—and Bartholomew G. Benneford never caused any trouble in Button Up. They did good things for this town. Because they were good people. The only trouble I heard about started with *your* ancestor, Max. Your great-great-great-grandfather Percy." Landon waited for his words to take effect. "That's right. We've heard about Percy *Want*morelandfieldshire. He sounded like nothing more than a selfish goat to me." Landon mispronounced the last name on purpose.

Max couldn't have appeared more stung and more riled if a nest of hornets had just attacked him. He flailed his arms wildly, howling. Landon shielded his sisters with his arms and drew them behind him. As he braced himself for Max's inevitable assault, the cabin pitched sharply and then fell back. They had stopped. Before any of them inside the cabin could react, more activity started outside.

"That's it. Right there. Man the ropes!"

Landon was feeling slightly dizzy from all the movement and emotions. Plus he was still reeling with the realization they had actually traveled back in time. . .*to 1861*. And was there something about that command— *"Man the ropes!"*—that was familiar, as well?

"Heave!"

Against the window the rope banged, taut. Creaking and groaning, the cabin was hoisted into the air, though only a foot or two from the wagon as it was towed out from underneath. There they hovered, held bumpingly in place by the partial framework of the corner of the House of Knowledge and Adventure, the future Button Up Library.

"Now down! Easy. . .steady. . ."

The cabin descended. The ride was gentle this time, although two of the walls were screeching in complaint as they slid along the stone of the library. They landed with a *thud*. The cabin's inhabitants all managed to keep their footing. When the rope slithered up the window like a coarse snake, Landon noticed the long view of the outside wall of the library. *Amazing.* It wasn't much to look at, and he decided then that Bartholomew must have predetermined the fate of the window. The side view of a stone wall simply couldn't compare to sunlight twinkling off a lake through the trees.

Chapter Five

Landon ducked as men appeared outside the cabin window. The men had a job to do, however, and didn't seem interested in peeking in the cabin. Dozens of men must have circled the cabin on three sides—guiding the opposing sides with the window and the bookcase, and pushing along the outside fireplace wall until the cabin's doorway was flush with the lobby. Since Landon had only seen the lobby with the cabin already in place as Bart's Reading Room, it was difficult to imagine a gaping hole there before.

No sooner had the cabin come to a standstill when the door clicked. Someone was coming in! Gasping, Landon crawled behind a tall crate and motioned for his sisters to follow suit. Landon glanced around anxiously for Max. Where was he?

Landon had passed right over the darkened fireplace before looking back. Feeling a mixture of relief and apprehension, he noticed Max was back in his crouching position beneath the mantel. If not for the barrel in the middle of the room, Max would be directly facing whoever might open the door. The good news was Max was nearly invisible inside his soot costume. Unless someone was looking for him or happened to notice those two blinking orbs, he probably would remain undetected.

A man stepped into the room, scanning from the bookcase to the barrel and fireplace across the crates and to the window. When his eyes grazed the crates, Landon felt his blood run cold. Thankfully Landon was peering around the edge of a crate, not over the top. Landon's pulse continued throbbing inside his ears until he feared the man might hear it. The man wore a long black suit with a funny, skinny tie looped below his neck like a bow. His dark, shiny hair was parted perfectly down the middle of his head, flopped over to either side. The man appeared to be sniffing as well as looking and listening. His eyes returned to the barrel. With a frown he spun on his heels and left the cabin.

An itch had invaded Landon's nose, and he held it until the door was safely closed. *"Mmnph!"* He plunged his face into his elbow to muffle the sneeze. Then he wiped his nose on his sleeve and looked up. To his amazement, Holly and Bridget were mincing toward the door.

He whispered urgently, "What are you two *doing*?" He wanted to shout at them.

Holly made a face and then waved him over. To Landon's relief, his sisters didn't open the door. They had stopped along the wall next to it. "Come here," Holly whispered. "I saw sunlight come through a couple good cracks here earlier. Let's see what's going on!"

Pressing his face between two logs, Landon found a gap just wide enough for his eye. Across the marble-floored lobby stood shiny black tables and chairs. The furniture style looked quite old, although these pieces appeared brand-new. They must have been the original reading tables, not yet moved into the collection room with the books.

A flicker of light caught Landon's eye.

Down the lobby to the right rose a stack of big, black iron rings like a tall, layered wedding cake. Candles spiked each black tier. A man also wearing a long-tailed black suit was lighting the top tier using an extended brass lighter similar to one Landon had seen used in his grandparents' church. Wick by wick, the collective blaze of burning candles grew.

"I thought the original chandelier had gas lamps," Holly whispered.

Landon nodded. "That's what Grandpa said. Looks like they were candles, though."

"Yeah," Holly said. She started quietly counting the candles.

"I wonder what happens to it?" Bridget was sitting low on her haunches like a frog, peering through a crack.

"To what?" Landon said.

"To this chandelier. If they switched to a gas one later, then they must have gotten rid of this one."

"It's a fire hazard, for one thing," Landon said. "I bet they replaced it pretty quick. I mean, I bet they *will* replace it soon."

Footsteps came from behind, followed by bad breath.

Max chuckled. "Fire hazard." He exaggerated the *f* and *h* sounds, mocking Landon while pouring extra-sour odor into the air.

Landon grimaced. "Don't you ever brush your teeth?" he asked, only regretting the question when Max opened his mouth and breathed even heavier.

The candles were all lit. The man with the brass lighter stepped back, snuffing it out. A chain rising from the center of the chandelier snapped to attention as the candle lighter motioned with his free hand to someone unseen to raise the chandelier. Up, up, up it went, eventually swaying ever so slightly, high above the middle of the lobby. Landon, Holly, Bridget, and even Max jumped when a burst of applause spattered through the high chamber. As they'd been watching the climbing chandelier, none of the children had noticed the group of men gathered across the lobby. The men were similarly dressed in black suits. Some had mustaches. A few wore round spectacles. Otherwise Landon would find it hard to distinguish one from another.

Holly snorted. "That's why old photographs are black and white."

Landon smirked. Bridget said, "What? Why?"

"Look," Landon said. "They're all dressed in black and white."

"Oh," Bridget said. "Then he'd fit right in, too."

Landon and Holly giggled, knowing Bridget meant Max.

"But they'd never see me," Max observed. "Because I'd blend right in with their shadows."

"No," Landon said. "You'd just look like a smudge."

His sisters giggled.

The noise of the applause echoed to a faint, spattering din. Then the group of men shuffled around, murmuring and squeezing into the hallway that led to the main collection room. When they fell quiet, Landon thought he knew what was going on. Feeling a thrill rising within him, he said, "This is it—the official opening of Bartholomew G. Benneford's House of Knowledge and Adventure." Without another thought, Landon turned from the wall to the door. But Max beat him to it.

"So long, Snows," Max said, stepping through the door. "Better luck next time!"

"No!" Landon heard his voice carry out into the lobby and bounce back again. He froze in the doorway, sure the men must have heard. But their attention remained fixed down the hallway. Even the chandelier lighter didn't break from his position.

Landon sighed heavily. Meanwhile, Max was creeping across the lobby toward the polished chairs and tables along the opposite wall like a black panther on his hind feet. Once at the furniture, Max went down on his belly like a black snake, an anaconda slithering silently beneath the tables toward his prey.

Landon hesitated only a moment longer before tiptoeing across the lobby and sliding under a table. He looked back and waved Holly and Bridget over. Watching his sisters scurry across the marble floor like frightened mice, Landon felt a mixture of humor and doom about their situation. What were they doing here in 1860s Button Up? What if they got caught? And perhaps most important, how would they get back?

Then there was Max, the most uncertain element in the whole equation.

Landon waved his sisters to him faster. They were breathing hard when they reached him. Feeling like a platoon sergeant leading his troops, Landon flopped to his belly and began to low-crawl toward the edge of the hallway. Max had left a black trail on the floor, which Landon and his sisters were unwillingly mopping up.

Max was pressed right up to the wall's edge, his face a mere foot from the candle lighter's legs. Landon reluctantly shimmied close to Max, trying to breathe away from him to avoid his smell. The girls came up next to Landon, the four of them barely fitting under the width of the end table.

Up close, the candle lighter's clothing appeared a little less black and much more worn than Landon would have expected. The man's shoes, in fact, were positively scuffed. A blend of scents wafted downward: hair oil, talcum powder, starch, a sort of musk or cologne. Landon had never been around such aromatic men. What they lacked in variety in appearance, they more than made up for in smell. And mostly they smelled good, which helped overpower the stench from the boy next to him.

A sharp tapping along the floor drew their attention. Landon couldn't see through the forest of legs, but he guessed the tapping came from a cane. And he guessed the user of the cane was none other than Bartholomew G. Benneford.

"Gentlemen, gentlemen!" A man's voice sounded clearly from down the hall. "You all know I have waited eagerly and most patiently for this day. Or shall I say *mostly* patiently."

A murmur of laughter accompanied a bobbing of heads.

"And now I will not bore you with much to-do about my love

and my passion for books and for nearly all things written and bound and wrapped within two covers to be opened and explored and enjoyed by readers young and old through the ages. Or with the minutiae of my appreciation and admiration of a book's power: how the essence of a single tome may escape only when a reader releases it, and how that essence—those words and those ideas and those images—may enlighten and entertain and edify and enthuse. No, no, and no. I will not delve into all that, as I know many of you—if not most of you—have precious other activities to occupy your time and your minds and your energies. Such passing fancies as politics, the pursuit of ever more commerce, and the compiling of ever more finances to fuel said fancies."

A few chuckles, though not as many, sprinkled the air.

"And so without any further ado. . .now who has the snippers?"

Laughter from one man in the group sounded snide, almost mocking. The man's voice came out in a whine. "Oh, that's fine. Now the old man's lost his snippers!"

An unpleasant silence followed before the "old man," whom Landon guessed had to be Bartholomew Benneford, exclaimed with great cheer, "Ah! Thank you, my good man. Snip! Snip!" The sound of actual steel blades echoed Bart's words. "I give you the House of Knowledge and Adventure. Open to the public. May the books within these walls find their way into readers' hands, hands that will release them to the world!"

"Hear! Hear!"

"Bravo, Benneford. Bravo!"

Applause spilled from the hallway into the lobby. Landon

was tempted to shout a *bravo* and to raise a cheer himself. But he held his tongue.

Lightning flashed with a *pop* and a *fizz*. Landon half expected thunder before realizing what had happened. A photographer had just shot a picture.

When a deep voice bellowed over the hubbub, Landon could have sworn he was hearing his own Grandpa Karl.

"All right, men. All right! For those so inclined to peruse, this library is now open. For those so inclined to stuff their faces and fill their bellies, refreshments are now being served outside on the portico."

"Thank you, Humphrey," said Bart.

Like a herd of hungry cattle, the mass of men jostled their way back into the lobby and headed for the entryway.

"Wait!" one man shouted, causing the herd to pause and turn their heads. "Howard Scoop with the *Button Up Bugle*."

"I know who you are, Howie." Bart's voice sounded tired yet amused.

"A couple questions for you, sir, on the day of your big event here. First, have you actually read all of those books in your collection?"

"Some of them twice," Bart responded.

A few men gasped at this revelation, while a couple of men chuckled knowingly.

" 'Some. . .of. . .them. . .twice.' Got it. Next question: Was it worth the wait to see your dream, your vision, finally materialize?"

An audible sigh. A thick moment of silence. Then, "Of course it was. Love, my good man, is patient. A dream without love and without passion is not a dream worth pursuing or waiting for. But some dreams and some visions are worth pursuing into eternity. That's how powerful love is, and how patient."

"Um, okay. You're still talking about books, right? About this library?"

Bart said evasively, "Somewhat, yes."

"Okay," Howard said. "No more questions."

The herd resumed the stampede for the refreshments. When the crowd had dispersed, Landon caught his first glimpse of his hero. Bartholomew G. Benneford looked very distinguished in his black suit with his mane of silver hair circling his face. Half-moon spectacles crested his nose. His cane leaned into the nook between a table and a wall, and the large "snippers" he had used were lying on another smaller, round table beyond that. A red ribbon lay on either side of the floor behind Bart, each half climbing to its respective wall from where it had stretched across as one tape earlier. Bart was holding what appeared to be a black leather book in one hand and an object Landon couldn't quite see in the other. Without warning, Bart glanced in Landon's direction. Landon had no chance to retreat from the old man's gaze. When their eyes met, Bart did the strangest thing. He set the book and the other object—it was something hard and maybe heavy—onto the table. Then he picked up his cane, looked at Landon, smiled, and fainted.

Chapter Six

As men in dark suits streamed back in from outside, sweating and puffing and asking questions about Bart's condition, Landon, Max, Holly, and Bridget crawled quietly and quickly backward beneath the row of tables along the lobby wall. Bridget bumped into a table leg, and Max knocked a chair out of place so that it screeched along the floor. None of the men in dark suits noticed the children, however. They were all concerned with the fainted founder of the library.

Landon watched anxiously as four men carried Bart to the far door. Sunlight streamed into the lobby around the silhouettes of the men until they had all filed outside. The door shut, and the light went out. It took Landon a moment to realize what was different. This door was solid wood, whereas the present-day library boasted double doors of glass.

The children were about to slide out from their cover when

a clattering sound froze them. The photographer had apparently stayed behind. A flash of light accompanied by a *pop* and a *fizz* burst from the hallway. Another clattering noise, and the man was hoisting his equipment rather clumsily into the lobby and then down toward the newly added cabin—Bart's Reading Room. Setting up in front of it, he went under a hood rather like a football referee reviewing a play. Flash! *Pop. Fizz.*

Bridget gasped.

Max was tiptoeing toward the photographer from behind. What on earth was he doing?

The man came out from under the hood and commenced turning a crank attached to his camera. Max had almost reached him when he turned around.

"What in tarnation! Where did you come from, urchin? Say"—the photographer wagged a finger—"aren't you Percy's boy Winkie?"

Landon stifled a giggle. *Winkie?*

The photographer put his hands on his hips, sizing Max up and down. "And where did you get those clothes? Whew! You get on out of here and clean yourself up."

Max stood his ground but only for a moment.

"That's it. Get! Shoo!" The photographer didn't want Max to get any ash near his precious equipment or his nice brown suit. He had to be the only man there not in black or dark gray except maybe the journalist Howard Scoop.

Max started down the lobby, but when the photographer turned his head, Max ducked down the hallway to the collection room.

Landon felt a tap on his leg. Holly said, "You see that? Max went—"

Landon put his finger to his lips. He mouthed the words, "I know." The photographer paused and turned his head. Landon stared, feeling his heart thumping inside his rib cage. The man slowly turned all the way around. He was looking right at them! Except then his eyes kept moving, skimming the tabletops and the stacks of chairs. There must have been just enough shadow from the flickering chandelier to conceal the motionless Snow children from the photographer's keen eye. When the man turned back around, collapsing the legs of the stand and clumsily hoisting the box camera away, Landon breathed a deep sigh of relief.

The photographer left, and the lobby itself seemed to sigh in quiet relief.

Now what was Max up to in the library?

"Come on," Landon said. He slithered out from under the table. Holly and Bridget followed him toward the hallway. It felt good to stretch his legs and his back. He was about to enter the hallway when the door to the library burst open. One man entered. Before the door swung shut, another man had caught it and pushed through.

"Now, Humphrey. You must be reasonable. Humphrey, wait!"

The first man, Humphrey, was striding headlong toward Landon and the hallway. If Landon ever felt like a deer caught in the headlights of an oncoming car, this was it. Something told him that Humphrey hadn't yet seen him, however. The man didn't appear to be really looking at anything. He was distracted, maybe even distraught. Lost in his thoughts. . .

Landon thought fast. "Back under the table!" he whispered as he slunk to the floor and backpedaled his way beneath the table. Bridget and Holly crowded in next to him. They watched breathlessly as Humphrey approached and then rounded the corner into the hallway. Landon gasped silently at the man's bearded and bespectacled face. It was like looking at Grandpa Karl.

Of course, Landon thought. *That's our relative—my great-great-great-grandfather.* He almost wanted to call out to him. *Hey, Humphrey! It's me. Us. Your great-great-great-grandchildren!* How odd would *that* introduction be?

Humphrey tapped the table with Bart's Bible as he passed by; then he disappeared into the collection room.

The other man was hot on Humphrey's heels.

"Cousin Humphrey. Now listen! Oh, all right. Let's talk in here, away from the crowd." The man went into the library.

Landon was still too dizzy from seeing his ancestor to wonder about what was going on between these two men. Like a slap in the face, he remembered who else was in the library with them. *Max.* Landon knew he had to go in after them to see what Max was up to. Not for the first time, Landon mumbled under his breath his displeasure over the grubby boy. Max was nothing but a nuisance.

On the table in the hallway, Landon discovered the Bible that would one day be his. It already looked surprisingly worn, although it certainly looked much newer than when Landon had received it on his eleventh birthday. He was tempted to flip through the pages and search for underlined passages, but there wasn't time.

Another object caught his eye. It was what Bart had held in his other hand and used to knock on the table. A fresh wave of dizziness swept through Landon as he recognized his very own dream-stone. Touching the engraved letters on the hard, creamy stone's surface, Landon thought he might faint himself. Holly interrupted his brief reverie.

"Someone else is coming, Landon. We'd better hurry."

"Hey," Bridget said, pointing. "That looks like your rock. And is that—"

"Yes," Landon said breathlessly, "that's my Bible, too. Although they're not mine yet."

"Wow," Bridget said.

A man's voice echoed from the lobby. "I believe he left his Bible here. He instructed he'd like it brought to him at the hospital."

With a longing glance at the Bible and the dream-stone, Landon prodded his sisters ahead of him as he rushed into the library and rounded the corner. He peeked back to see a man lift the Bible and carry it away. A mixture of happiness and sadness flooded Landon's heart as he remembered Grandpa Karl's story about Bartholomew G. Benneford. *He had his Bible brought to him at the hospital, where people read to him.* Landon again saw Bart's face smiling at him. Landon sniffed back a tear.

A shout arose from deep within the library, across several tall rows of shelves. In the midst of this excitement, Landon still noticed the wonderful smell of thousands of books. Thick paper and leather bindings. Also the polished wood of the shelves and the parquet floor. Under different circumstances, he could sit in here a long time and merely absorb the atmosphere. Knowledge and adventure indeed.

The shout was repeated. "No! It will not happen."

The two men and Max were nowhere to be seen. Landon half crouched and led his sisters across the floor to the reference section in the center of the room. With the reading tables and chairs still out in the lobby, little remained to disrupt their path through this part of the room.

The giant dictionary known as the *Book of Meanings* held its place of honor atop an ornate stand amid shelves holding other lesser dictionaries, encyclopedias, and atlases. Landon allowed himself only a few seconds to run his fingers along the book's edge. "Someday you'll grow a lot bigger," he whispered lovingly, "and I'll climb your pages."

Knowing this library like his own house, Landon crept to a row of bookcases near the back corner of the room, where the men's voices were heard.

"How can you be so disagreeable with me, Cousin?" This was the man who had followed Humphrey into the building. His voice sounded nasal and pinched. "I have the certificate right here in my hand. It reads, 'Good Sir,—' "

"I said no, Cousin Percy," Humphrey interrupted. "And I meant it." He wasn't yelling anymore.

If Humphrey and Percy are cousins, Landon pondered, *and one is our great-great-great-grandfather and the other is Max's, then that means. . .* He didn't want to finish the thought. A sour taste filled his mouth, and he swallowed. *Max is related to us. Ugh.*

"But Cousin Humphrey, you are most certainly being unreasonable," Percy whined. "Does it not make wiser sense to have the deed drawn in the names of *two* families rather than only *one?* The Snows *and* the Westmorelandfieldshires? As they say, 'Two families are better than one!' " He laughed a screechy "heh-heh, heh-heh" sort of laugh.

"No," said Humphrey in a very low voice. "Now if you would be so kind as to depart from my presence, I have some reading I would like to attend to. Alone."

"Po-eh-try," Percy said in a mocking, childish manner. "Snow-ah-tree." He giggled as if he'd made a marvelous joke. "See? I can compose rhymes as fancy as any in these *books.*" Percy sniffed.

Humphrey sighed.

"Think of the money," Percy continued in a pleading voice. "A place like this could generate hundreds—"

Humphrey roared, "Enough!"

Landon and his sisters flinched.

A book slapped shut.

"But this library is *privately* owned," Percy whimpered. "Admission can be charged. Think free enterprise, dear cousin! Think entrepreneurship!"

Humphrey sounded tired. "Bartholomew G. Benneford's House of Knowledge and Adventure will remain privately owned—by him. He is still alive, you know. When the unfortunate time of his passing should come, then I will inherit ownership of his beloved collection. And I mean to keep it and care for it as he would. It is, and will continue to be, public in practice even as it remains private in ownership. This is Bartholomew G. Benneford's library. Those are his wishes. As they are mine. And I pray that those entrusted after me will carry on his legacy, and his alone."

Wait a second. The library would be passed down to Humphrey? To Landon and Holly and Bridget's great-great-great-grandfather? Then it was in their family. And if it stayed in their family from then on, that would mean it was in Grandpa Karl's name now. Landon could hardly contain himself. He looked around at the towering walls of books and the winding staircase with multilevels known as "the Tree." With a thrill, Landon thought, *This is in our family. The Button Up Library—the BUL—belongs to our grandfather!* No wonder Grandpa Karl knew so much about its history and its founder. And. . .could it be chance, mere circumstance, that a secret passageway led from Grandpa Karl's own study, from behind his bookcase no less, to a bookcase in Bart's Reading Room?

Landon muttered, "Grandpa Karl's known everything all along." He smiled briefly but then frowned. "It's not just property that Max's family wants; it's this place. The library. And here's Percy trying to add his name to Bart's will."

Again Landon glanced around, this time looking for Max. Where was that stupid kid? *Blending in with the shadows.* Anger and revulsion pricked Landon's heart. If Max did anything to Humphrey or to this library, there was no telling what Landon might do in response.

One man suddenly breezed by, his coattails flying. The other man gave chase, and for a moment Landon thought Percy was going to tackle Humphrey right there in front of them.

Bridget was clutching Landon's arm. Holly leaned close, panting. Landon tried to press the three of them back into the shelves. Their brush with people in the past was getting a little too close for comfort.

Blessedly, Humphrey quickened his pace. Landon, Holly, and Bridget kept low and followed from row to row. Humphrey stopped short of the hallway, causing his pursuing cousin to bump into him from behind.

Humphrey pointed. "Get out. Leave me in peace."

Percy placed his hands on his hips, his elbows jutting like chicken wings. "This isn't your library. You can't make me—"

"Now!" Humphrey bellowed. Everyone else flinched.

Dropping his arms and bowing his head like a scolded puppy, Percy skulked from the library. He swung back with a sneer and cried, "I'll get you for this, Humphrey Snow. If not you, then your family. Mark my words. Someday—"

"Out!"

Percy disappeared down the hallway.

Humphrey turned and surveyed the vast collection room. Raising his eyes to the ceiling, he closed them and folded his hands.

"What's he doing?" Bridget whispered.

"Looks like he's praying," Holly said.

As Humphrey continued praying, Landon felt his anger and unease soften and fade. A fresh sense of peace and, strangely, *love* was filling his heart. For his great-great-great-grandfather. For Bartholomew G. Benneford. And even for this place, the specialness and sacredness of it.

For the first time, Landon likened the stillness of the library to the peace and quiet of a church. *All it took was a prayer,* he thought.

Humphrey was raising his arms as if offering something up. Himself? The library? Bartholomew Benneford? *Cousin Percy?*

Landon sighed. Why did Percy have to be so selfish and whiny? If Percy had gotten his way and gotten his family name on the deed, the library would have belonged to Max's grandfather *and* Grandpa Karl. But the Westmorelandfieldshires would not have been satisfied with joint ownership. What if they had somehow obtained sole ownership of the library along the way? Landon shuddered. Then it would belong to Max's grandfather, not Grandpa Karl. And that would mean it might have been passed down to Max.

Max.

As if reading Landon's thoughts, Holly whispered, "Where did Max go?"

Humphrey's eyes were still closed. He stood before the entrance to the collection room looking exhausted. Landon felt sorry for him, and he wanted to go over and give him a hug.

"There he is," Bridget hissed. "Up there!"

Max appeared on one of the Tree's top branches. He moved quickly from the catwalk to a wall of books. Then, remarkably, he began *climbing down the wall* like a spider. Descending from shelf to shelf, the boy had obviously done some scaling in his day. Landon couldn't help being a little impressed beneath his mounting rage. *He's probably climbed these walls before*, Landon thought angrily. Max had shimmied up the chimney. What else had he climbed in Button Up?

Max lost his footing, and three books came sailing down. *Bam! Bam! Bam!* They smacked the floor. Humphrey's eyes snapped open. He looked toward the noise. Then his eyes began to climb the shelves up the wall.

"Oh no," Holly whispered.

With about fifteen feet to go, Max himself fell from the wall and landed on the floor with a thud. Humphrey saw the boy. Surprisingly, he reacted by briefly closing his eyes and sighing. Then he left the library. Landon heard his great-great-great-grandfather mutter a single word as he entered the hallway: "Winkie."

"He thinks it's Percy's son, just like the photographer did," Landon said.

"What do we do now?" Holly asked.

"My knees hurt," Bridget complained.

Max kicked a book on the floor, sending it whizzing into a wall. Laughing, the boy jogged through the library toward the hallway.

Unable to take anymore of his foolishness, Landon stood and shouted, "Max!"

Max only half turned. "Humphrey's going down," he said cruelly, continuing toward the exit.

"Oh no, you don't." Landon broke into a sprint as he spoke. He heard Holly say, "Come on!" to Bridget behind him.

Max turned the corner and went into the hallway.

Landon plunged in after him.

Holly and Bridget were running after him.

Humphrey stood in the center of the lobby waiting for them. Max plowed right into him. Humphrey merely plucked the filthy boy away by the shoulders, holding him at arm's length.

Landon skidded to a halt. Holly and Bridget plowed into him from behind so that they all crowded Max and Humphrey. Humphrey's eyes widened. As he and Landon looked at each other, Landon half expected Grandpa Karl to smile and remove his old-clothes disguise, telling him this whole time travel thing had been some sort of trick.

But the two only stared at one another.

Meanwhile, Max was wriggling and yelping in Humphrey's firm grasp. "We'll get you back for this, Snow." He glared at them wildly. "All of you. . .Snows."

"Get us back for *what*?" Bridget asked. "You're the one who spit on our grandparents' property."

Humphrey glanced from Landon to Bridget. Then to Holly. "You're. . .Snow children?"

They nodded. "And you're our great—"

Before Landon could explain, a creaking sounded from above, followed by several spatters of hot wax striking the floor around them.

"Say good-bye, Snow. My father *will* inherit this rotten library once old Bart and you are dead!"

Another boy stood atop a table near the wall. He was holding a pair of clippers—the shears Bart had used to snip the red ribbon in the hallway. He looked astonishingly like Max, except he was dressed in funny knee-length pants and a rough but clean shirt. His hair was slicked back, shiny.

It was Winkie, Max's great-great-grandfather.

They could have been twins.

Winkie had already partway sliced a rope that secured the chandelier's chain to the wall. That's why the chandelier was rocking overhead.

"Who are *you*?" Winkie pointed at his soot-smudged twin.

Max stared back. Then he looked up. "Wait," he pleaded. "I want to kill them, too!"

The wickedest grin Landon had ever seen spread on Winkie's face. "Come on."

A drop of hot wax struck Humphrey's shoulder, and he released his grip on Max's shoulders. In an instant, the boy flew to the tabletop to join his great-great-grandfather. Together, wearing matching grins, they each took hold of a handle and brought the blades together on the remaining strands of rope.

Landon only had time to make one move. With all his might he lunged at his great-great-great-grandfather, shoving the bewildered man out of the way as the chandelier came crashing down.

Chapter Seven

When the explosion of fire and wax and smoke had settled, Landon found he was huddled with Holly and Bridget. They were trembling, but they were okay. They were alive. A huge bonfire rumbled and roared before them. But something was different. Something had changed.

Landon looked up. *The sky.*

It was dark above the bright glow of the fire. And still higher, beyond the rising scrim of smoke, there appeared stars.

"We're outside," said Landon numbly.

"And it's nighttime. . .again," said Holly.

Bridget stuttered, "I'm cold."

Landon huffed out a breath in a laugh. She couldn't possibly be *cold*, not with that bonfire burning like a furnace. But his own vaporous breath seemed to indicate otherwise. As Landon exhaled upward again, watching the puff from his mouth rise and vanish, he realized he felt a distinct chill in the air—coming from behind. It was like he was in the middle of a strange sandwich, hot in front and cold in back. The cold air prickled and plucked at his back like a dozen flexing cat's claws. It felt good in a way. Much better than the searing heat at his face. Landon found himself taking a step back, to be embraced by the tickly cold until his entire body involuntarily shivered.

Something clutched his elbow. Not a cat's claw of cold, but his sister, Holly.

"Landon, stop."

Something in her voice made him obey. Landon stopped. Holly was tugging at him, drawing him forward. Bridget let out a whimper.

"Look behind you," said Holly.

Her voice sounded eerily empty of emotion yet full of something else. Landon felt he was on the verge of something big, wondrous, and mysterious. Slowly, he turned from the giant fire to face, well, nothing. There was nothing but open space and inky black sky speckled with stars. The fire made a sound like a rippling flag behind him, and Landon felt a thrust of warm air at his back like a huge heated hand pushing him forward. He took one step, caught himself, and stared down into the abyss. At first it was like looking at a mirror image of the sky, perhaps reflected in a vast, still sea. But there were not as many stars as up above. And the dots glowed brighter than their heavenly counterparts. No, those weren't stars down there. Neither was it a big black sea. In an instant, Landon knew what he was looking at, although he had no idea where they might be.

"It's a valley," said Landon staring in bewilderment. "Full of little fires."

"Or not-so-little fires," said Holly. She reached out to clutch his right elbow, while Bridget took hold of his left hand with both of hers. His sisters' grasps made Landon feel more secure in one way: as if he were anchored to the top of this precipice. On the other hand, he realized if one of them tripped and stumbled over the edge, they'd most likely all go in a chain effect.

"What do you mean, 'not so little'?" asked Landon as he squinted against an upward gust of cool air.

"Well, look how far away they must be. They might be huge up close, as big as this one is."

Impossible, thought Landon, though he didn't say it. Could all those dots of light really be giant fires? How far up was this ledge he and his sisters were standing on?

Bridget squeezed his left hand. "What happened? Where are we?" She shivered. "Landon, I'm scared."

Me, too, Landon thought. "It seems we're between a rock and a hard place," he said, trying to sound cheerful. "Or more like between the dark and a hot place." His joke fell flat. Landon sighed, drawing his sisters closer to him and putting his arms around them. "I don't know, Bridget. Something about this place seems oddly familiar. But at the same time, I sure don't recognize it. I guess we have to believe we've been brought here for a reason."

"What happened to the library?" said Holly. "I mean, do you think the chandelier really crashed in the lobby? And then would the whole building catch on fire?"

Landon hadn't considered this. Though they had been inside the library perhaps only minutes before, the whole scene now seemed a distant memory or even a dream. Had they really journeyed into the past and seen Bartholomew G. Benneford and their forefather Humphrey Snow? Another thought sent chills up Landon's spine. Had Grandma and Grandpa Snow's neighbor Max actually traveled back in time with them? As much as Landon especially wanted that part to have been merely a dream, he couldn't shake the feeling that it was true.

The next thought was perhaps the most frightening of all.

If Max had gone back to old Button Up with them, then where was he now?

"What's wrong?" asked Holly suddenly. "You shivered."

"Oh," said Landon. He was about to lie and say he was cold, which wasn't a complete lie, anyway. But he decided to tell the truth. "I was just thinking about Max."

"Oooh, I don't like him," said Bridget.

"He tried to kill us," said Holly bluntly. "That mean little—"

"Yeah," said Landon, "but where is he *now*? Since he came from the future like us, either he's still back in Button Up in 1861, or—"

"No," said Holly. "He couldn't be." She squirmed as she glanced warily around.

"Well," said Landon, "unless he was somehow transported back to present-day Button Up, these would be the only two options."

"I can see why Grandma Alice hates them," said Holly.

"She didn't say she *hates* them," Landon said.

"She didn't use that word, maybe, but after meeting Max, I think I—"

"Don't say it." Landon squeezed Holly tight. "It's not good to think like that."

"He tried to kill us," Holly argued.

"Yeah," said Bridget copying the hard edge in Holly's voice. "We could have been killed."

Landon swallowed. Was it ever okay to hate or to seek revenge? It didn't feel right. Or at least it didn't feel *good*. As he tried to put Max out of his mind for the moment, a vision appeared to rise up before his eyes. Was he actually seeing a close-up scene from the valley, or was this only his imagination? In either case, what he saw, in a glimpse, in a flash, was a tall stone wall. Like something you'd see around a castle. Or a fort.

"Fort Sumter," Landon said suddenly. He blinked, and the image of the wall faded. The dark, distant valley returned, spangling with specks of light.

"What?" asked Holly.

"What?" repeated Bridget.

Landon explained. "Remember Max said it was 1861 when Bart's House of Knowledge and Adventure was completed? That was the year the Civil War started, when a shot was fired at Fort Sumter in Charleston harbor." His sisters remained quiet, either contemplating what he said or merely feeling bewildered by it. Landon continued. "Sounds like an oxymoron, doesn't it? A civil war. It's a paradox."

"All right, you lost me," said Holly. "What's an oxygen moron?"

"Is it the same as a pair of ducks?" said Bridget hopefully.

Landon felt befuddled himself. "A pair of—? No. An oxymoron is just something that doesn't make sense. Like war is violent, and *civil* means *polite* or *courteous*. But a polite or courteous war doesn't really make sense. In the American Civil War, though, civil meant it involved citizens of the same country. A country at war with itself. Or people fighting their own people."

"Like a pair of ducks," said Bridget, "fighting each other."

Landon smiled. "Sort of. Sure."

"You're right," said Holly thoughtfully. "People fighting their own people doesn't make sense."

"Why were they mad?" said Bridget. "What were they fighting about?"

"Slavery," said Landon. "Some people wanted to own slaves, and others wanted to set them free."

The fire hissed and whipped in the wind behind them. Landon reflexively leaned forward, bowing with his sisters. Then he teetered back, and they all stood upright.

"We'd better look for some shelter for the night," he said. "Maybe in the morning we'll be able to find a way down."

"Do you really want to go down there?" asked Holly.

Landon gulped. "I don't know if I *want* to, but something tells me we might have to."

"Why would we have to?" asked Holly.

Landon gazed across the vast valley toward a dark, unseen horizon. "Because to get home, I think we'll have to cross to the other side."

Holly didn't ask, and Landon wouldn't have known how to reply anyway. It was only a feeling, but a strong one, that that's what they would have to do. He'd learned to trust feelings like this because they were often put there by Someone else. As the three children turned to walk carefully along the edge of the cliff and then around the fire, just beyond its blistering reach, some words came to Landon that he'd read in his Bible in Grandpa Karl's study: *Come now therefore, and I will send thee unto Pharaoh, that thou mayest bring forth my people the children of Israel out of Egypt.*

Landon stopped in his tracks, causing Holly to bump into him. Bridget trudged on a few steps alone and then whirled around, startled.

"Wha—"

Landon raised his hand. Slowly, he turned back, gazing past Holly to the dark, distant land dotted with lights. "Couldn't be," he muttered.

"Couldn't be what?" Holly whispered.

Landon felt far off in his thoughts. Holly's voice seemed to come from another realm.

"Egypt?" Landon slowly shook his head. "This doesn't look like Egypt, does it?"

"Uh, no," said Holly. Bridget had returned and was clasping Landon's hand. "Though it's hard to tell from this height," Holly continued, "I don't think that's sand down there. Isn't Egypt mostly desert? And no pyramids or sphinxes."

"Sphinxes," Landon said mindlessly. "No sphinxes."

"It's trees," said Bridget simply.

Landon half returned to the moment. "What?"

"Trees," she repeated. "There's a forest down there. A big one."

Landon stared at his youngest sister. Firelight glimmered from her shiny brown eyes. Something seemed right about what she was saying. Yet—

"How do you know?" Landon asked.

Bridget's eyes squinted, though she wasn't looking at something. She was lifting her nose. She was *sniffing*.

"I smell them. The trees. And some of them are burning."

Suddenly, the vision returned. Landon saw the tall wall of stones and, around it, trees. Big, glorious trees! But patches of them were burning. Crackling, shrinking, dying inside hungry fires. Strangely, however, the fires didn't spread to the surrounding trees. Each bonfire seemed self-contained, burning only its patch to the ground. Something dark and evil was happening down there, Landon knew. He decided he didn't need to tell his sisters this, however.

"All right," said Landon feeling a twinge of disappointment. "So we're not in Egypt. Which only means I have no idea where in the world we are." He led the way this time, with Bridget and Holly in tow. Beyond the bonfire, the ground rose up still higher. They were not merely on a cliff, but had been deposited on a ledge jutting from the side of a mountain. Its peak was indiscernible in the darkness. Landon only hoped to find a dry cave or some other means of shelter and perhaps some brush to lay down for a nest. He didn't want to stray too far from the fire, because that was the only place they "knew," and once they found their campsite, he planned to build a little fire of their own for warmth, borrowing a flame or two from the big bonfire.

They didn't find a cave, but they did come across a somewhat concealed nook beneath a rock overhang just large enough for three kids and a fire.

"Why don't you see if you can scrounge up some sticks and leaves?" Landon told his sisters. "Sticks for a fire and leaves to lie on. Don't stray far from this spot. Otherwise we might not find it again."

"Where are you going?" asked Holly. Landon detected a trace of worry in her voice that seemed to say, "Don't leave us!"

"Back to the fire to get some for us. I'll holler out, 'Hey!' and you guys shout back to me—in case I have trouble finding my way." Landon grinned to reassure the girls.

"What if we don't hear you?" Bridget said, her voice conveying even more concern than Holly's.

"Then sniff for me," said Landon. "You seem to have a pretty good sniffer there." He touched Bridget's nose and smiled. She smiled back weakly.

As Landon started off, trying to follow the same path they had taken, Holly called after him. "Landon?"

He turned his head. "Yeah?"

"Hurry!"

"Okay!"

Landon headed back down the mountain. The path before him grew brighter as he drew nearer to the bonfire. Glancing back only once, his sisters and the covered nook were already veiled by sloping ground and darkness. "I'll find them," Landon said to himself. "No worries."

A voice cried from somewhere off to his right. "He–e–e–e–lp." It sounded weak and was followed by a low moan.

Landon froze, feeling his heart bump inside his chest.

"Who's there?" he called in the direction of the voice.

"U–u–u–n–n–h–h–h. . ."

Landon thought he recognized the voice. If it turned out to be who he thought it was, his question about whether the mean boy from Button Up had come through the portal or not would be answered. Landon wasn't sure he wanted to find out. Maybe he had only heard the wind whining. Besides, he really did need to hurry and get some fire back to his sisters.

But the voice moaned again. A boy's raspy voice. And Landon knew it was real. *He's here,* he thought with a sigh. After only a moment's hesitation, Landon turned and hiked toward the pitiful groaning. Though he knew who he was about to see, Landon would not have guessed the condition he'd find him in.

Chapter Eight

Maximillian Westmoreland was hanging upside-down from a rope, his left ankle ensnared in a tightened noose. Max's hands were dragging on the ground, except when he used them to push against it and momentarily raise himself in a handstand. But then he would collapse, or dangle, exhausted. And he'd moan. Landon watched the wretched boy try desperately to bend himself up and scratch at the rope clasping his ankle, only to flop downward again like a strung fish. Max's right leg was bent at the knee, limp, except when he struggled and used it to kick at the air as if trying to find some invisible foothold.

If it were anyone else, Landon would have reacted immediately to help release the prisoner from the trap. But as he watched Max thrash about and then go limp, something held Landon back. He knew he couldn't leave Max there. Yet it somehow seemed fitting that Max had gotten himself into this fix.

The rope ran up to a single branch that extended about fifteen feet over the ground from the burnt remains of a tree. It was a fairly grisly sight, worsened by the flickering strobe effect of the fire. Landon wasn't sure whom he felt sorrier for, Max or the charred, fire-ravaged tree.

"He–e–e–ey!" Max's face came into view, lighting up when he saw Landon. "He–e–eyyy!" Max's body slowly twirled, forcing his head to follow. He whipped his neck around to find Landon, while his body caught up, turning. The effect was owl-like and rather grotesque. Landon didn't know whether to grimace or to grin.

"It's you!" Max let his gaze drift as his head turned away. After another moan, he said, "I'm gonna be sick." When his face returned, he locked on Landon with pleading eyes. "You gonna help me?" Max's eyes closed and his face contorted. "Uuunnnhhh."

Something like anger stiffened Landon's limbs and then propelled him to the hanging boy. Landon's first impulse was to grab Max and hold him up, but that would only provide temporary relief. And he'd still be upside down. He needed to be cut down. As Max's body swung around, Landon noticed he was sweating. Profusely. He could see it and smell it. And then Landon felt the searing heat from the flames himself. Reflexively he stepped back.

"Blades," Max sputtered. "Scissors." He groaned and twirled. He appeared to be weakening.

Landon was about to say "What?" when he noticed the large shears stuck into the ground. Blackened and dirty, the silver blades cast little reflection. Landon stared at them, thinking first of Bartholomew G. Benneford opening the House of Knowledge and Adventure with a happy *snip*, and then of Max using them to cut the rope that held the chandelier aloft—

The rope. Landon eyed the taut, twisting line holding Max. *Of course.* It was the same rope, although how it had found both Max's ankle and this poor tree was a mystery.

Max had grown quiet.

Landon stepped toward the blaze, squinting against the heat, and reached out to touch the scissors' handle. Ow! Hot. He jumped back and looked around for a sturdy stick. After snapping a number of weak, brittle branches over his knee Landon found one that would do the trick. Moving quickly, he thrust the branch through the opening in the scissors' handle, grabbed it on the other side, and tugged. The blades stuck stubbornly for a moment before giving way and trailing Landon as he stumbled backward with the stick. Laying the scissors on the ground, he used the stick to beat them. Some black crust came off. Eventually the metal was cool enough to touch.

The next problem was reaching the rope. On his tiptoes, Landon could barely extend the long shears enough to nip the rope with their tips. After several strained, unsuccessful snips, Landon drew back and rested the blades on the ground, leaning over exhausted. He needed something to stand on. "A chair would be nice," he muttered. It would be especially nice to sit on after he finished this rescue project. What was there he could stand on?

Looking up at Max's boots, another idea came to Landon.

The boots were black military combat boots. The laces at the top of the left boot had come partially undone. It looked as if Max had tried to untie them. But the rope's cinch at his ankle was too tight around the lower boot for it to come loose from his foot. Unless. . .

Landon stood, took a deep breath, and reached up with the shears as if he were about to trim a tall hedge or prune a tree. Working the point of one blade under the laces above the rope's coil, that is on the lower part of Max's boot, Landon began to chew through them one by one. The boot was loosening but not quite enough. When Landon reached the boot's toe, he prayed it wasn't made of steel. Gripping the black leather between the blades and pushing the scissors' handles together as hard as he could, Landon felt sweat streaming from his body.

Finally, something gave way, and Landon fell back, careful to keep the cutting instrument away from his body. He sat, panting, staring in disbelief as Max continued to hang upside down like a rag doll hastily plucked up by a child.

The bonfire whooshed and crackled. Sparks rose into the night sky. Max didn't moan or groan. Landon wondered if the boy was dead. Landon was too physically fatigued and emotionally drained to feel anything. He could hardly lift his arms, let alone try to hoist the shears up for another go. It was perhaps the bleakest moment of Landon's life. But he only felt numb.

And tired.

He wanted to cry. But no tears came. When he swallowed, the dryness of his throat made him choke and cough. Then

Landon moaned, and he groaned, and he wanted to cry for help.

A split second before it happened, Landon thought he heard something. Or perhaps he only sensed it. In either case, something flicked inside his mind, and he knew that it had worked. The boot remained in the noose, but Max's foot slipped through. His body fell headfirst with two soft thuds. He lay there face-up, having fortunately curled the right way and practically done a somersault. Half his body was bathed in firelight, the other half in darkness. The left foot was nearest the fire. Max's sock, if he'd been wearing one, had apparently slid off, as well.

Hot foot, Landon thought to himself. Letting the shears drop to the ground, he mustered his remaining strength to drag himself over to Max's body, grasp it under the armpits, and drag it away from the fire to the opposite side of the tree. Though Max's head had just taken a shock from the fall, Landon placed his hand behind it and laid it gently on a soft patch of earth. Soft, Landon discovered as he lifted his hand, because it was a mound of ash. Collapsing beside the motionless boy's form, Landon pushed himself against the tree. He leaned his head back against the hard wood and looked at the dark, smoky sky. This was it, then, he thought. He could no longer move. It seemed that not only Max, but Landon, too, was about to die.

Landon's eyelids drooped.

He only wanted to rest.

He was thirsty, though.

What about Holly and Bridget? They were waiting under that rock, probably shivering, watching for their brother's return. He was supposed to take back fire to keep them all warm.

And now he hadn't even saved Max, this boy who seemed to hate Landon and his sisters for no reason. So their ancestors had argued a century and a half ago. What was that to Max and Landon or even to Landon's grandparents? It was silly is what it was. But this wasn't so silly now, sitting here next to a dead boy, dying of thirst and exhaustion and heat and smoke himself.

I should have left you hanging there, Landon thought as if Max could hear the words. *If you were just going to die anyway.*

Landon's chest convulsed, and a dry, painful cough followed. He felt his face tighten as if on its own. He certainly had no strength to move it. The tightness hurt, but it only grew tighter.

I'm sorry, Landon thought to Max. *I'm sorry I didn't respond faster. I'm so sorry!*

Landon coughed again. His eyes half opened and then closed. Directing his thoughts heavenward, he thought it again. *I. . .am. . .so. . .sorry.*

Sorry.

Sorry.

Landon's right eye suddenly burned. And then his right cheek burned, followed instantly by coolness. From somewhere deep inside him, a single tear had found its way out.

A low, rasping moan. Landon felt nothing. He heard the moan as if it came from outside his body. Perhaps he was dead now, floating above himself as a spirit, hearing sounds coming from his former body.

"U–u–u–n–n–h–h. . ."

Landon's eyes half opened. Without moving his head—he couldn't move it even if he'd wanted to—he looked at the boy's body lying near him. Something was different.

"U–u–u–n–n–h–h. . ."

Max was moaning. Which meant he was breathing. Which meant he was alive.

Landon's focus blurred as his eyes welled up. It felt like someone was squeezing his face like a sponge, wringing out more tears. He sobbed forcefully and silently. When the tears trickled into his mouth, their saltiness tasted bitter, but their wetness felt sweet.

The night passed, and Landon awoke with a splitting headache, a parched mouth that tasted like smoke, and his neck and back so stiff they felt as rigid as the tree that was supporting him. Landon moaned, and then he groaned. Then he remembered the body next to him.

Except it wasn't there.

Max was gone.

Landon caught his breath. Had it all been a terrible dream? For one wishful moment, he wondered if he might be back beneath the willow tree on the hill on his grandparents' property in Button Up. As much as he had been anticipating another adventure through the library, now he was hoping it wasn't real after all. The thought of drinking several glasses of water in Grandma Alice's kitchen tortured his throat. It hurt even to swallow.

Unwillingly, Landon found himself moaning again. He realized he must sound like Max had sounded last night. Max had been caught by a rope. Landon had been trapped by exhaustion and smoke. And now, dehydration.

"Wah—ter," Landon whispered, as if the spoken word might somehow soothe him. "Waaahhh—teerrr. . ."

Slowly leaning his head forward, Landon surveyed his surroundings. In the gray, ashen earth, footprints danced around the tree. Well, *one* actual footprint—a left foot—alternating with the print of a boot. A combat boot. Max. What had he been doing before he apparently took off? And where had he gone?

Despite his stiffness and pain, Landon lurched his upper body away from the tree. *Bridget and Holly.* Might Max have found them? What would he do to them? Landon's heart was racing. But if Max still wanted to hurt them, why hadn't he done anything to Landon while he was out cold against the tree?

Landon's head dully reeled. *Because I saved his life.* Had he done the right thing? Now a new ache pushed its way into his brain—and his heart. He was worried for his sisters.

It was time to move.

Rising quickly, Landon had to close his eyes and press his hand to the tree for balance. Head rush. He felt like the Tin Man starting out rusty and stiff. Each flex and extension of his limbs took great effort, shooting streaks of pain into his body. He had only reached the edge of the bonfire heap, which was all burnt out save for some quietly orange-glowing embers, when he heard a rustling from the nearby trees. Landon stopped, his entire body throbbing like his heart. It was easy for him to remain still. In fact, it almost felt restful to hold this position.

The rustling quieted. Now there was only heavy breathing. Panting, actually, like a dog.

Or a *wolf.*

The creature's yellow eyes reflected from the underbrush. Then they disappeared. The wolf was on the move.

Landon turned his head, trying to follow the sound. It was difficult to see much. Everything nearby was coated gray or black from the smoke and soot. And the wolf, Landon guessed, was either gray or black. It was perfectly camouflaged. And now it was quiet.

Landon breathed. The sky was even gray. Overcast. Not dark or heavy with rain—*Oh please, please rain!*—but merely filmy with smog.

The wolf seemed to have left. Something caused Landon to turn and look back, and he was surprised to notice the rope was missing from the tree. It also appeared that the split left boot was gone. A strange thought occurred. Could Max have stepped on Landon's head to reach the tree limb that had held the rope? It seemed absurd, yet Landon wasn't sure he would put anything past that kid. And it would explain why it felt like someone had slammed a ramrod down Landon's spine.

I'm going to kill him, Landon thought.

He peered to his right, past the cliff's edge and across the hazy valley. Beneath the smog lay a vast forest spotted by dead bonfire heaps that made Landon think of a disease that causes patches of hair to fall out. But each of these ugly spots was perfectly round. What was happening to the forest? Looking at it stirred both a feeling of longing and of dread. Something was destroying the trees.

Toward the far end of the forest—could it be? At first it merely blended with the grayness of the sky, like a gray sea with no horizon. But its shape gave it away. Landon gasped anew, and then he choked on the sudden intake of air. He was staring at a faraway wall complete with towers. What were they called? Turrets? No. Those were on castles and were covered. These towers stood open and, though Landon couldn't distinguish the details from this distance, he guessed they had that up-and-down tooth shape across the top, with open-air windows beneath. *Battlements.* That's what they were called. Like rook pieces on a chessboard.

"Battlements," Landon muttered hoarsely, pleased that he had come up with the proper word. As he stepped into the sparse, dusty wood, however, he wondered why on earth such an immense wall marked by massive battlements stood along this forest. What was it protecting? Could it be hiding something? Or more likely, what was on *this* side of the wall that it meant to protect—someone or some people—from?

Who might these people be? Where were they?

The valley and the wall felt as far away as a fairy tale, so Landon wasn't too terribly concerned about their inhabitants, if there were any, at the moment. But the whole scene was rather curious. Thoughts of his sisters and Max and the mysterious wolf crashed into Landon's brain and spurred him onward. Pushing through his aches and pains, he climbed the slope. At the sight of the rocky overhang, he held his breath, letting it out with a sigh of relief when he saw Holly and Bridget huddled together beneath it.

Something seemed wrong, however.

Rather than crying out in joy, which would have come

out as a mere squeak anyway, Landon pressed his lips together and crouched behind some bushes. His sisters were staring at something. They weren't moving or making a sound. He couldn't make out their faces, but he sensed it. They were afraid. Movement opposite the girls' cavelike nook drew Landon's eye. Out stepped a large gray wolf balancing something between its jaws that looked like a big stick.

Chapter Nine

As the wolf approached Holly and Bridget beneath the overhang of rock, Landon's mind did cartwheels over what to do. Should he try to scare it away? Should he tell his sisters to run? Should he charge the wolf and tackle it if necessary, risking his own life to save his sisters?

Wait a second. . .

Landon squinted. Something about this wolf was familiar. The thought of tackling it reminded Landon of a time when *he* had been tackled by *it*. The wolf had pinned him to the floor of a cave on the Island of Arcanum—to say thank you for Landon's lifting the Arcan curse from all the animals imprisoned there. And then the wolf had helped Landon as he had battled Chief Arcanum on the beach. The gray wolf. *This* gray wolf.

Landon uttered his name. "Ravusmane."

The wolf paused in midstep, one leg bent in the air, dangling its paw. It turned its head and growled. The deep rumbling from the wolf's throat reverberated within Landon, arousing both fear and delight. Landon knew this was the same wolf. But it didn't seem the wolf had yet recognized *him*.

The stick dropped from Ravusmane's jowls, and he continued to growl at Landon, now baring his teeth.

"Ravusmane," Landon said, boldly standing. "It's me." His voice, he realized, was extremely rough and raspy. He must not sound like himself at all. But surely the wolf must recognize him. Didn't he? Ravusmane's snarl did not subside. Instead, his curled-back lips began to drip saliva to the dirt. Had the wolf gone mad? What should Landon do?

Holly and Bridget were staring at him, too. And they appeared no less afraid at the sight of him. What in the world was going on?

"Holly! Bridget!" The effort was too much, and Landon bent over, hacking. He looked up at his sisters. "It's me. Landon." He forced out the words with all he had in him. This was all too bewildering. He needed to sit down again. He needed water.

"Landon?" It was Bridget. Oh, her sweet little voice came as music to his ears. Landon could only cough and hack in response as he half sat, half collapsed to the ground. He feebly raised his hand and waved, hoping they could see it above the bush. He felt like he was waving a white flag.

The wolf snuffled and snorted and then resumed its low growl. It seemed a little less ferocious and threatening but no less cautious. Eventually, it came over and sniffed at the bush. From beyond, another voice called out.

"You leave him alone, wolf! That might be our brother!"

Might be? Landon's head was swimming. Amid the confusion over what was going on with the wolf and his sisters, Landon was beginning to put something else together in his head. If this wolf *was* Ravusmane, and he was pretty sure that it was, and if Ravusmane had traveled aboard the ark with the rest of the rescued animals from the Island of Arcanum, which Landon was fairly certain that he had, and if the ark had returned to Wonderwood with them, which is where it was reportedly headed when Landon and his sisters departed from it aboard another ship at sea, then that forest must be Wonderwood.

The world began to spin around him.

But if that is Wonderwood down there, Landon mused as he stared unseeing at the ground, *then where are the giant Whump Trees? And where did that wall come from? And—*

Oh, dear heavens. They can't be. It can't be. But how? And when? No—it doesn't seem possible. Could this really be the mountain beyond the foothills at the far end of the valley? What happened down there?

Landon felt his upper body swaying and then falling. He hit the dirt and rolled onto his side. Without moving his lips, he felt and heard a soft moan come out through them. The next moan, however, didn't even make it past his throat. That is, until a big wet tongue began to lick his face. Landon closed his eyes, unable to fight or resist. The next thing he knew, he was being dragged by the back of his collar—he could feel the wolf's muzzle along the nape of his neck—and then deposited on a harder, rougher surface. Slowly, Landon opened his eyes. Not far above him arched a ceiling of glistening stone. It was glistening because it was wet. Landon willfully opened his mouth, parting his sticking lips. And he prayed. He prayed for one drop to fall from that ceiling into his mouth. One drop of liquid, and it didn't matter how it would taste. Just one drop—

"It *is* him." Three heads loomed over him. *Out of the way!* Landon willed. They were blocking his source of hydration. "I can't believe we thought he might be Max."

Max? Why on earth?

"Well, he sounded like him."

"And he looked like him, kind of, with all this dirt on him."

"It's not dirt, Bridget. It's ash."

"Ash?"

"Soot. You know, from fire and burnt wood."

"Oh."

Oh, thought Landon. *Ohhh!* He'd been covered in ash just as Max had been when they found him in the fireplace inside Bart's cabin. And his voice? Rough and raspy. Landon almost wanted to laugh. Or cry with relief at understanding. Either one would hurt too much. And he didn't have the strength. There was one thing he needed to ask for, however. He licked his lips, but his tongue felt like a thick, dry finger rubbing against rough skin. Even the stickiness had dried.

The word barely made it out. He hoped it was understandable. "Wah—ter."

Ravusmane growled as if he intended to say something. He wagged his broad head to part the girls. Then he disappeared. Then he returned. Something clattered on the stone floor nearby. *The stick.* Ravusmane bobbed his head. He seemed to be indicating the ceiling. The glistening, wet ceiling.

Yes! Landon wanted to shout. Yes! *Run the water down the stick into my mouth!*

"What is it?" asked Holly. "You want us to use the stick to. . . to what?"

Ravusmane clamped the stick in his teeth and tilted his head. He wagged back and forth, waving the stick like a drum major's baton. It almost struck the ceiling, but not quite. Landon stared at a sparkling spot of liquid. So close and yet so far.

"Here," Bridget said, taking the stick from the wolf. Ravusmane yielded. Bridget commenced waving the stick as Ravusmane had done. It stirred the air, but nothing else was happening. Landon wondered if he might get hit in the head. Ravusmane made a yelping sound, which startled everyone, and then he pointed at the ceiling with his snout.

"Here," said Holly, "let me try." Bridget handed her the stick. With one swift movement, Holly whacked the stone ceiling. *Smack!* Immediately a stream of water poured onto Landon's face. It was like opening a spigot from heaven.

After drinking down gulps of water until his belly felt like an inflated balloon, Landon closed his mouth and relished the refreshing splashes on his face. No shower had felt better, even after playing outside all day. Movement was restored to his arms, and Landon rubbed his hands in the water and then wiped his face. As quickly as the outpouring had started, it suddenly stopped. *Drip.* A wet strip remained on the stone ceiling.

"Are you all right, Landon?" Holly asked. "What happened?"

"Help me up," Landon said.

His sisters each grabbed an arm and hoisted up their brother. It felt as if he had just returned from a nightmare, rousing from a very strange dream.

"Thanks," said Landon. "How did you do that?" He was glancing at the bubbles of water clinging to the rock not far above his head. He looked at Holly as if she'd performed a magic trick.

Holly gestured toward the wolf, who had positioned himself outside their little nook as if standing guard. Or simply to give them a little family time together. Holly picked up the stick. Except it wasn't a mere stick, but a full-length staff of slightly twisting wood, complete with a gnarled head worn smooth to fit a grasping hand.

Landon's eyes grew wide. "Is that the same stick?"

Holly and Bridget looked at each other. Finally, Holly said, "We had a very strange night last night. Scary, too. But mostly weird."

Landon frowned. Then he nodded. "Me, too. You go first. Wait. Tell me about the stick. And weren't you afraid when Ravusmane"—Landon glanced at him and then lowered his voice, though he was sure the wolf's perked fuzzy ears could still hear him if he wanted to—"when the wolf came at you just now? I was trying to get him away from you."

"Scared? No, not really." Holly didn't sound totally convincing.

"*I* wasn't," said Bridget. "I was happy to see him again!"

Ravusmane sat up straighter, and Landon thought he heard him sigh.

"You mean since we saw him on the Island of Arcanum?" asked Landon.

"No." Bridget shook her head. "Since last night. He came by a few times—"

"Seven," interrupted Holly, ever the specific number girl. "Seven times."

"Yeah," said Bridget. "I think he was checking on us. Making sure we were safe. We pretended to be asleep until this time."

"He came right in and sniffed us the first time. I"—Holly looked at the floor, a little ashamed—"I thought he was going to eat us."

"I *told* you he wasn't," Bridget said, flaring her eyes at Holly. "Even if he was really hungry, he would never eat us."

Landon couldn't help glancing out at Ravusmane again. The stately wolf only sniffed at the wind.

"And the stick?" Landon touched the tapered end of the staff, and a thrill like a gentle electric current ran up through his arm. Then the wood merely felt like wood again. Landon looked up. "And the water?"

Holly looked at the length of wood. It was too long now to waggle or twirl like a baton. "I don't know." Her voice sounded distant. "During the night, it was too dark to see. But we knew the wolf had visited us—eight times, now, including this morning. And, well, we heard other sounds or voices, too."

Bridget had a far-off look, and she nodded. Suddenly, she smiled.

Landon squinted at her. "What, Bridget? What are you smiling about?"

"Animals," she said softly. "We heard animals talking."

Landon's first thought was that maybe his sisters needed a good splash of water on their faces, too. But his second thought quickly trounced the first. There was only one animal he had ever heard speak before—

"Melech?" he said excitedly. "Was it—"

But Holly was shaking her head. "I don't think so. Could he even climb up here?" She glanced at her brother. Reading his expression, she added, "Sorry, Landon. Pretty sure he wasn't here, though. I would recognize his voice, too. Young Landon." She smirked, but it was really a half smile. There was no mockery in her voice.

A hot blade touched Landon's heart at those words. *Young Landon.* That's what his favorite horse and best friend always called him. A new desire sprang up inside him. He wanted to get down to the valley. . .

"But if not Melech," Landon said, savoring the sound of the horse's name, "then what animals could—"

Bridget's hand shot out, her finger pointing. "He did," she said. She was pointing at Ravusmane.

The hairs on the back of Landon's neck tingled. For some reason, he knew the wolf was listening, though he was still facing outward from the stony alcove. Landon swallowed. "He can *talk*? But how can he—I mean, why didn't he talk to us earlier? Or why not *now*?" Landon stared at the wolf's backside expectantly, knowing Ravusmane could hear him. Yet Landon really didn't believe the creature could actually speak. Instead, Ravusmane emitted a low but pleasant growl. If he were a cat, it would have been a purr.

Landon looked at his sisters. "Uh, that's not speaking, exactly. I thought you meant he talked in English."

A breeze flowed through the tiny space, humming and whistling simultaneously. Ravusmane's fur flickered like grass. For a moment, Landon thought back to the grass on the hill beneath the willow. And then to the pages turning in the Bible and the words he later discovered to be underlined in green. "Exodus," Landon whispered, the word getting sucked silently into the wind.

Ravusmane turned his broad, gray head almost fully back, like an owl. When the gaze of his amber eyes found Landon's, the wolf's mouth opened and closed. Landon was sure he had heard a word, though as soon as it sounded in his ear, it, too, was gone with the wind. "Yes," Ravusmane had said. Then he turned away to stare out at the world.

The breeze calmed, and it was quiet.

"Did you hear that?" Landon shifted his gaze from one sister to the other. "Did you hear him?"

Holly and Bridget both stared. "I heard the wind," said Holly, "and. . .and I think I heard the trees." Her eyes fell and she looked sad.

"I heard the animals," said Bridget. Her eyes appeared moist, and Landon wondered if she was about to cry. "And—" She couldn't speak for the trembling of her lower lip.

Landon waited, blinking. Was he fighting back tears of his own? He felt something, though he didn't understand what it was. Only that it was something sad. He touched Bridget's shoulder, feeling the tremor stirring her from within. "What else do you hear, Bridget? It's okay."

She shook away violently, though her reaction didn't seem directed at her big brother. "No! It's not okay! It's not right!"

Landon began to feel frightened. He was about to touch Bridget again, when he stayed his hand. He sighed and waited. Undetected, Ravusmane had entered the nook, padding right up to Bridget. He gently nuzzled her side, which under other circumstances would have produced giggles of delight (so long as she wasn't scared of him, which she clearly wasn't). Bridget clung to a tuft of fur along the wolf's great neck, and immediately she relaxed, though her sobs continued in wobbly waves. Finally, after a few loud sniffs, Bridget looked up, imploring Landon with her eyes.

"I heard people," she said. Her big brown eyes closed, and her dark wet lashes dripped. "Like Hardy and Ditty and her parents and Wagglewhip and Battleroot and. . .and lots of others."

Landon felt his insides twist like the wood of Vates's walking staff.

Vates's staff!

It was all Landon could do to keep from standing up and knocking himself out against the overhang of rock. He felt pain inside—others' pain—though he didn't understand why. *They're crying out for some reason. Something bad is happening or has already happened.*

But now he also felt a spring of hope *inside*. This was Vates's walking staff Ravusmane had brought to them. That didn't explain how it had shifted sizes or had produced water from the rock, but suddenly those questions didn't seem as important as they had a minute ago. Vates had sent his staff to them, Landon was sure. *And this means that Vates knows we're here.*

Now a new string of questions presented themselves. Why hadn't Vates come himself? What kept him back? Was it his old age? Or was he in danger? Landon didn't need to ask his sisters too many more questions about the previous night. What he had just witnessed showed they were indeed hearing many things. Strange, wondrous, fearsome things. And frightening though this was, Landon also knew it meant something else. He and his sisters had been brought here for a reason. The Auctor, who was the Creator of their world and of Wonderwood and of every land in the universe, was putting a plan into effect. Landon remembered the words that had first gained him entrance into the extraordinary realm beyond the Button Up Library: *And it shall come to pass afterward, that I will pour out my spirit upon all flesh; and your sons and your daughters shall prophesy, your old men shall dream dreams, your young men shall see visions.*

Sons *and daughters* will prophesy. Landon was sure glad to have his sisters along.

Chapter Ten

On the way down the mountain, miraculously it seemed, Landon, his sisters, and Ravusmane passed an apple tree. But not without stopping to pluck some fruit and eat it. The tree seemed miraculous because it was in the right place at the right time, just when they all needed some nourishment. It was also quite curious because it had grown in the middle of a large ash heap. And it must have sprouted quickly. So there it was: a leafy green tree decorated with red apples surrounded by burnt, crumbled logs and soft, coal-colored powder. Strange.

The fruit tasted good. Landon's limbs felt stronger again for eating it. He burped aloud, and that felt good, too.

But theirs weren't the first footprints to dent the pile of dust. Two boots had reached the tree trunk previously. Landon had already been telling his sisters about his nightmarish experience finding Max.

"What do you think he's doing now?" Holly asked. She had an apple to her mouth but wasn't chomping it. She was bent over, studying Max's boot prints like a detective searching for clues.

"Who knows?" said Landon almost carelessly. He was enjoying eating too much to concern himself over Max at the moment. "Maybe he's gotten lost in the woods. Maybe he'll never come out again." Landon was getting full, but he took another bite of apple anyway. He couldn't help still feeling some spite toward the boy. With his free hand, he massaged the back of his neck. Then he touched the top of his head. Had Max really used him as a footstool to reach the other tree? Landon rolled his head around and grimaced, although his neck was feeling much better.

Holly stood upright, tossed aside the remains of her apple, and placed her hands on her hips. She looked up into the tree and giggled.

Landon looked at her. "What is it? What's so funny?"

"He was hanging upside down from a tree," Holly said. Another giggle rippled from her.

Landon frowned at first. There was nothing funny about what had happened last night, including the way he had found Max. But then simply because it felt good to do so, he allowed a little laugh to bubble up. It really did feel good. So he let another laugh come out. He glanced at Bridget, who hadn't eaten much. She was standing at the edge of the heap near Ravusmane. They both faced the sparse woods ahead, which led to the bottom of the mountain.

Bridget held Vates's walking staff, which was a foot taller than she was. Her other hand rested on the wolf's head, who didn't seem to mind in the least. She could make a good veterinarian some day, Landon mused. She certainly had a way with animals. She loved them.

They were difficult to see from here, but from higher up, Landon had noticed the swell of hills that lay before them— "small bumps" that preceded the vast valley. They were the foothills. And there were many of them to traverse. The journey down the giant mountain had already been taxing. Thinking about how far they still had to go was difficult.

A pang tugged at Landon's heart. He wished Melech were here. It would be great to see his friend again. But there was another more selfish reason. *Melech could carry all of us on his back.* Well, with the exception of Ravusmane, that is. The wolf could clearly take care of himself.

Landon's giggles died. He went to join his youngest sister and the wolf. When he heard Bridget's voice, however, he paused, standing behind them.

"So this creature, the so-called Flying Fire, comes out each night and burns up more of the forest? That's awful. Why does he do it?"

Ravusmane growled and whined. Bridget shook her head.

"That's no reason at all. That's just sad. And all the people are locked up?"

The wolf lowered his head and made a humming, purring sound. It made Landon's heart hurt.

"Slaves," said Bridget, sighing. "To the Arcans. Well, really to the fire monster. Sounds like they're all slaves to him." She raised and lowered Vates's staff twice. *Thud, thud.*

Ravusmane lifted his head. Slowly he turned it half around, much as he had done outside the nook by the overhang earlier. Owl-like. He looked at Landon as if he'd known he'd been listening in. The wolf looked sad, that was certain. And there was something else. His deep amber eyes spoke something to Landon that was more personal and disturbing than even talking about slaves and a fire monster, whatever that was. At least, this is what Landon felt gazing back into Ravusmane's eyes.

The wolf sighed, his body visibly deflating, and turned away. Bridget scratched his head between the ears as if she didn't know Landon was there.

"Hey, Bridge," said Landon, stepping alongside her. "Ravusmane." He glanced at the wolf. "Were you two talking? I thought I heard something."

Bridget looked at him. "Oh, it's awful, Landon. Everything's awful." Her eyes glistened, but something seemed to have hardened inside her. She wasn't about to cry. Her focus, Landon could tell, was on something else.

"What's awful?" said Landon. "Wait. Were you really talking to him? I mean, was he talking to *you*?" It felt strange talking about Ravusmane while he sat right there on his haunches.

Bridget's brown eyes crinkled slightly at the corners, hints of a smile. "Yeah. He told me everything. At least, all the bad stuff that's happened here." Her smile faded.

"What's going on?" Holly came alongside Ravusmane, and he snorted.

"Bridget and Ravusmane have been talking," said Landon skeptically. "Both of them. To each other."

Holly looked more believing than he was. "Really? And?"

"Wonderwood's been taken over by the Arcans," Bridget blurted. "They left the island and followed the ark here after we rescued the animals."

"No!" said Landon, appalled.

"Yes," said Bridget. "And now not only the animals, but the people, too, are slaves. They're all kept behind the wall. And it's worse. There's a monster destroying the forest. They call him Flying Fire—"

Ravusmane raised his head and howled, causing Landon and Holly to jump. Bridget merely looked at the wolf and continued.

"Or *Volucer Ignis.*" She eyed her brother and sister. "Which means, uh, *flying fire.* And it sounds like he's really the one everyone's afraid of, including the Arcans."

Landon frowned. "You mean they're not on the same side? This creature and the Arcans?"

Ravusmane whimpered, and Bridget nodded.

"They are," said Bridget. "They're all on the bad side. But Volucer Ignis rules through fear. So everyone—every*thing* it seems—fears him."

Holly looked at the mound of dark dust around the apple tree. "And he's destroying the forest. . .with fire?"

Ravusmane snuffled. Bridget nodded.

"Yes."

"But why is he only doing these bonfires, one at a time? Why hasn't he set the whole valley ablaze?" Landon tried not to think about this too much, tried not to feel the emotional impact of such a thought. He was staying objectively curious.

After a moment of quiet, Ravusmane leaped forward without warning. Growling and huskily barking, he tore into the woods, leaving the children in stunned silence. Ravusmane's snarls receded among the trees. A long minute or two later, panting sounds preceded his reemergence from the wood. He came back and sat down almost as if nothing had happened, except his heavy breathing continued.

Only then did Landon realize his knees were trembling. *Don't do that, wolf!* he wanted to cry. Instead, as he scanned the trees for what could have possibly provoked Ravusmane, Holly spoke.

"Th–that wasn't him, was it?" Her tremulous voice betrayed her own fear.

Ravusmane responded with a snort that sounded like a low "Yip."

Landon stared at the wolf. "Did he just say, 'Yep' or 'Nope'?" His heart was racing.

"No," said Bridget. "That wasn't the monster. Apparently, he only comes out at night. Or"—she looked at Ravusmane—"at *dusk*, just before night." Bridget lowered the staff toward the woods. "That," she stated assuredly, "was a lone Arcan."

Landon gasped despite himself, his eyes again scanning the columns of tree trunks. After catching his breath, he said, "Did you kill him, Ravusmane? Is the Arcan dead?"

Ravusmane raised and dropped his forepaw with a shake of his head. Landon understood this, much to his dismay.

"You let him get away? That—thing?" Unpleasant images of the Arcans on the Island of Arcanum sprang to mind. "Why?"

Ravusmane murmured, and Bridget interpreted. "A dead

Arcan means a dead—" She broke off.

Holly put her hand on Bridget's shoulder. "A dead animal?" she offered.

Bridget loudly sniffed. Her head lowered, she shook her dark curls back and forth. "No. If an Arcan is killed, then one of the valley people will be killed." A loud sob burst out. Poor Bridget was trembling. Whatever hard edge she had earlier was whittled away. She cried freely, teardrops falling to the dirt.

Landon stepped closer and embraced her, and Holly did the same. The three of them stood quietly together, holding one another and sniffling. This was almost too much to bear. Eventually, Landon looked over at Ravusmane, who appeared unmoved. If anything, the wolf seemed more statuelike than ever. Thinking of those stern looks the wolf had given him, Landon said aloud to Bridget, knowing Ravusmane would also hear, "How do we know all this is true? We haven't seen anything. And we didn't see this Arcan out in the woods. What if something else is going on and this is just a story to scare us?"

Bridget stiffened and then stepped away. She appeared much older than her nine years when she turned and glared at Landon.

"You don't believe this is real? You're the one who said you thought something bad was happening here, remember?"

Landon blinked. His mind went blank. Bridget had never stood up to him like this before. What had gotten into her?

Bridget heaved a sigh of exasperation. "On the hill by Grandma and Grandpa's, you said you saw smoke and that something bad was happening—or had already happened—in Wonderwood. And it's true. And here we are."

Bridget's hard edge had returned—with a vengeance.

Landon had to look away. His little sister's normally soft brown eyes had grown intense. He had seen that vision, if that's what it was, of smoke. And yes, of course he remembered what he'd said and felt. But still, all they had actually seen here were some strange bonfires, a distant wall, and now Ravusmane. And what was with those strange looks the wolf was giving him? Landon didn't know whether to feel guilty or distrustful.

Landon took a deep breath and looked at his littlest sister. "Bridget." Another deep breath. "How can you understand him?" He didn't have to gesture for her to know he was referring to Ravusmane. "You were having a whole conversation earlier. I heard you talking to him. All I heard him say was 'Grrr' and 'Growl' and 'Bark!'" Landon swallowed, surprised to find his heart pumping so fiercely. He glared at Bridget and waited.

She glared back, and then she softened. After a few wondering blinks, she began to look more herself again. A soft, sweet little girl. Landon almost felt sorry for being so harsh with her. But he found out he needn't have.

"Vates said you might react this way."

Now Landon stood really dumbfounded.

"What?" He wanted to throw his hands in the air or shake something or pound on something. Instead, he merely crossed his arms and repeated the question. "What?"

Holly intervened, speaking softly. "Yeah, Bridget. What are you talking about? When did you speak to Vates?"

"I didn't," said Bridget. "But he told Ravusmane everything he was to tell me, including that you might not believe it,

Landon. Even after seeing the stick grow into the staff, you might not believe."

Landon closed his eyes a moment. He was feeling rather dizzy all of a sudden. He opened his eyes and sighed, keeping his arms crossed. He cleared his throat. "And—*ahem*—what else did Vates tell Ravusmane to say to you?" Landon looked askance at the wolf.

"Only that the reason you might not believe everything is because you're becoming an adder—" She made a face. "An address or an amendment." She blinked. "Or something. Something that might keep you from seeing what you believe."

Landon huffed. "You mean, from believing what I see?"

"No." Bridget shook her head firmly. "From seeing what you believe."

Landon had never felt this way before about his littlest sister. Or about Ravusmane or Vates, for that matter. What did they know? What could Bridget possibly possess that he didn't? She couldn't even pronounce certain words. It suddenly seemed that the whole world misunderstood him. Seeing what you believe. This was plain silly is what it was.

"Landon."

It was Holly. At least she was pretty close to his age. She might still understand.

"What?" said Landon sharply. He couldn't help it. He didn't have time for any more foolishness.

"I think Bridget meant to say *adolescent*."

Landon straightened himself even taller. "What?"

"You're almost a teenager. You're not a little kid anymore."

"That's right. But what does that have to do with any of this?"

Holly looked at Bridget, and Bridget looked at Ravusmane.

At first the wolf did nothing other than twitch one ear—his right ear—slightly inward and then out. Like a little radar checking the mountainside. Then he got up, stepped next to Bridget, and sniffed the staff up and down. Landon crinkled his face, wondering if the wolf was about to lift his leg and do something disgusting. He was part of the canine family, after all.

But Ravusmane did no such thing. Instead, he looked up at Bridget. When she looked kindly back at him, he made several gentle yipping sounds. Bridget nodded, and then Ravusmane sauntered back to his sentry position and sat down.

Landon wanted to laugh or scoff, but he couldn't. He whispered to Holly, "Did you understand that?"

Holly shook her head. Then she said, "I believe Bridget can, though." She raised her eyebrows at Landon. "I heard animals last night, too. It was like a dream. All dark. But I knew they were talking. I don't remember what any of them said, but this morning when Ravusmane came to us, I *knew* that he could talk. I don't know how else to explain it. And I don't understand it."

"Is it the staff?" asked Landon, suddenly wanting to reach out and grab it. "When you hold the staff, you can understand him?"

Bridget handed the striated stick to Landon, and he took it. It was all he could do to keep from shouting, "Speak!" to Ravusmane.

"That's just to show you that it was Vates who sent Ravusmane to us. Understanding the animals has to do with believing not only what you see, but also what you hear."

Landon closed his eyes and concentrated on the breeze. When

he'd heard it that morning and remembered the flipping pages in his Bible, he'd thought of the book of Exodus, whispered the word, and then heard Ravusmane say, "Yes." Did he believe the wolf had actually spoken to him? He could hear and understand Melech, couldn't he? Why was it so hard to believe the other animals could speak to them, too? Could speak intelligibly to *him*?

Because they're animals, you idiot, part of Landon's brain said.

Something deeper inside his heart was beginning to stir, however. He was in Wonderwood, after all, where so many magical and inexplicable things had happened to him. Why stop believing now?

Because I'm not a kid anymore. I have to grow up some day.

But was that really it? As Landon listened to the breeze, he realized it wasn't the moving air he heard so much as the rustling leaves and the swaying branches in the wood. He felt like this was all a test. Vates was putting him to it or through it. Were his sisters in on it, as well? Or was he just growing paranoid?

Feeling the gnarled head on the staff and clutching it firmly, Landon opened his eyes.

"I don't want to believe the bad things," he said finally. "I want to forget about them or at least pretend they're not there." He sighed, feeling his breath float away with the wind. "And if I don't believe the bad is really there—if I ignore the darkness—then I'll—" Something caught in his throat. Landon swallowed and cleared it. "Then I'll miss the good things, too."

"Do you want to keep believing, Landon?" Bridget asked him hopefully.

Landon looked at her and smiled. "I do," he said. "I want to keep believing. . .like you do."

"Me, too," said Holly, a funny look spreading over her face. "I want to believe like that."

" 'Atta boy. 'Atta girl," growled a voice. "I might just tackle you both and lick your faces!"

Landon and Holly both looked at Ravusmane and grinned. It felt less surprising than Landon would have expected, hearing a wolf speaking in plain English. It felt really as if he should have been hearing him speak like this all along.

"Well, you already licked me today," said Landon playfully.

"Yeah, blech. That was different."

"And back on the island. I'll always remember that."

Ravusmane nodded. "Yes. My own ideas have grown since then. Meaning what I believe and what I see. And who I hear." He got up from sitting and turned to look at the children. "Vates has been teaching us all about the Auctor. With him around, there is always hope, even though it appears the enemy is taking over."

"So, what's our next move?" Holly asked. "What can we do to help?"

"We need to get to the wall and get inside."

Landon leaned on the staff. "And then?"

Ravusmane looked at him with something of a smile, which appears rather odd on a wolf. "And then we need to get back out again."

"With all the animals," said Bridget.

"And the people of the valley," said Holly.

"Precisely," said the wolf.

Chapter Eleven

The three Snow children followed Ravusmane into the wood and farther down the mountain. Landon was still uncertain how he could understand Ravusmane's speech now, when only a half hour ago he'd heard only whines and growls. As Ravusmane padded easily along through the trees, he offered an explanation.

"Because you believe," he said simply.

Landon brushed a low branch out of the way. "Because I believe," he echoed, frowning. "Because I believe you *can* talk?"

The wolf glanced briefly back at him. "Precisely."

He likes that word, thought Landon. *Precisely.*

"So when I wasn't hearing you, or at least, not hearing you speak words, I wasn't believing you could talk." Landon readied himself for the word.

Ravusmane leaped a fallen log without breaking his gait. "Right," he said.

Landon smiled.

Ravusmane continued. "You were seeing a wolf, an animal that you *knew* couldn't speak your language. So you were unable to hear it."

Landon nodded. This seemed to make sense. Sort of. Then he thought of something. "But back on the island after I'd broken Chief Arcanum's curse, I tried speaking to all the animals, but no one could understand me. And then Melech had to interpret for me. He could understand me, *and* you, and he could speak to both of us."

"Melech is a horse of great faith," said Ravusmane. His step slowed and he sniffed at the air. Or maybe he was pondering something. He moved on around a bush, and Holly and Bridget caught up from behind, panting and then complaining Ravusmane was moving too fast for them.

"We'll rest soon," Ravusmane said to the girls. Resuming his discussion with Landon, he said, "The truth is, back on Arcanum I couldn't yet speak to you. I didn't know your language then."

Landon paused, watching the wolf and then Holly and Bridget walking quickly on. "What?" he called into the forest, and then broke into a jog after them. "What?" he repeated as he caught up, coming alongside Ravusmane. "How did you learn it?"

"Guess."

At first Landon thought of Melech. The horse obviously spoke fluent animal and human. He was about to say Melech's name when two words popped into his head and he changed his mind. *Great faith.*

"Vates," said Landon, feeling his heart leap at the mention of his old friend's name.

Ravusmane barked, startling Landon. For a moment Landon feared he'd only hear wolf sounds again from Ravusmane. Would he ever speak human again? Had Landon's own faith been that short-lived? He glanced at the wolf, keeping pace with him as the earth leveled before rising into the first foothill. They had reached the base of the mountain.

Bridget's voice wheezed as she raced past, only to slow down again until Landon was beside her. "He said, 'Precisely,' in case you're wondering." She paused, catching her breath.

Ravusmane stopped several feet ahead and then turned back. He wasn't breathing hard at all. He was just getting warmed up. He nodded toward Bridget and then, much to Landon's relief, spoke in clear English. "She's right." He looked back at Bridget with a pleased squint.

Landon looked from Bridget to Ravusmane and then back at Bridget. He leaned over, resting against his legs. "You mean"—*breath, breath*—"you could understand that? I only heard a bark. How—"

"She understands animal, too." Ravusmane's pleasure was evident. "Your sister is bilingual."

Bridget whimpered.

Ravusmane gazed at her seriously. "Yes, we can rest a moment here. But only a moment." He looked at Landon, who was gaping at both of them in astonishment. Holly, too, was watching with her mouth hanging open, although it may have only been because she was winded. "We will need to crest the hills by midday. The Arcan I scared away earlier?" He paused, waiting for a response.

Landon and Holly stared and nodded.

"He will surely reach the wall by then. And then—" Ravusmane sighed and glanced up.

Landon raised his eyebrows. "And then. . .what?"

Ravusmane growled, a deep throaty rumble that sent shivers up and down Landon's spine. The wolf's teeth were bared. Landon had never seen him look so ferocious.

Bridget made a high-pitched whining sound, and Ravusmane stopped, though he didn't utter a word. Finally, Bridget interpreted for him. "Flying Fire," she said softly. "Volucer Ignis."

Landon was thinking of the huge bonfire from the night before and all of the fires they'd seen from the mountain ledge dotting the vast valley forest. Suddenly, he remembered Max.

"Did you see anyone else last night?" he asked Ravusmane. "A boy a little taller than me, all covered in ash?"

Ravusmane gazed at him. "No. Someone else? There is another human in the wood?"

Landon sighed. "Yes. His name is Max. He came from—" He paused, realizing he was about to say *the future*, but that wasn't quite right. "He came from the same place we did," said Landon. "From another world that's like this one but also different."

"Hmm," Ravusmane said in what sounded like both a human hum and an animal purr. "That is interesting. Vates did say something about another. . ." His voice trailed.

"Another?" Landon prodded. "What did Vates say about him?"

Ravusmane sniffed the air. He gazed upward. For a moment

it appeared he was about to howl. But Ravusmane remained silent. Landon sensed that, beneath the thick gray fur, the wolf was tense. Finally, Ravusmane relaxed slightly and looked at each child in turn.

"Vates said the other would not be good for us." His ear twitched. "Or for you."

A breeze stirred the trees, and the whole forest seemed to be muttering dark secrets.

"I say we go," said Holly abruptly. "Remember how Max was listening to us when we were talking under the willow tree? I think we should move on and not talk much until we're someplace safer."

Landon couldn't help looking at the trees, eyeing them for a suspicious figure in the form of a boy. *A dirty boy from Button Up who shouldn't even be here.* Anger flared up inside him. Gritting his teeth, Landon nodded. "Holly's right. Let's keep going."

Ravusmane looked at Bridget and offered a questioning whine. Bridget responded with a sharp, "Yap!" which had Landon and Holly giggling as they started up the hill. Hearing the wolf and his littlest sister communicating in animal talk as they mounted the rise and started down no longer bothered Landon. In fact, he found it comforting. He and Holly trailed behind Bridget and the wolf. And whenever Bridget made a doglike noise, Landon could only smile proudly at her bouncing brown curls.

Bilingual, he thought. *Imagine that.*

After climbing and descending about a dozen hills (eleven actually, not twelve, Holly would have people know), they came to one final small mound, a mere bump in the earth that preceded the line of trees marking the edge of the vast forest. Before reaching the tiny hill, Landon sensed something familiar about it. What was it? Then he realized it wasn't the hill he recognized, it was the view beyond it. He felt like he was stepping back into an oft-recurring dream.

"I've seen these trees before," he whispered. "I've been here before—more than once." As they walked up the hill, Landon could hardly keep from jumping up and down. He wanted to shout for all the valley to hear, but instead he spoke just loudly enough for his sisters. "This is Vates's place, his home beneath the hill!"

Holly and Bridget both stared at him wide-eyed. But as they stepped down the hill, Landon's excitement subsided. Something was different. They shouldn't have been able to walk down this side of the hill. It should have been a sheer face with a door and two windows facing the woods. Landon's mind raced, and he had to bite his tongue to keep from thinking aloud. *What happened? Where did Vates's house go?*

And then his mind leaped to even darker thoughts.

If Vates's home had been destroyed, apparently blotted out to appear it had never even existed, then what had become of its owner? Ravusmane had brought them Vates's staff, which Landon now held tremblingly in his hand. The wolf had said it was to prove that the old prophet had sent him. But how long ago had he sent him? *What had happened to Vates?*

Landon was about to ask Ravusmane, not caring about keeping quiet anymore. But the wolf had taken off into the trees, weaving in and out down the tree line like a gray needle stitching a hem along the forest's edge. If Landon hadn't known where to look for him, Ravusmane's presence might have gone undetected once he'd reached the trees. The wolf could be stealthy as a shadow when he wanted to.

So Landon waited anxiously, trying to still his hammering heart as he poked and prodded the grassy incline. He couldn't believe it wasn't here. Twice he stopped to gaze at the hills on either side, in case he might have mistaken this one for Vates's place when it was somewhere else. "No," he muttered. "This *is* it. I know it is. It's like it was all a dream now, though. The bookshelves, the tea and crumplets, the pumpkin pie, the room farther in with a chessboard table, and the bunkroom. . ."

"He's checking for something," Holly whispered at Landon's shoulder. She was gazing toward the trees, barely shifting her head as she followed Ravusmane with her eyes. "Making sure the coast is clear. We've stopped here for a reason."

Bridget stepped between Landon and Holly, squeezing herself in. "It's a safe house," she murmured, allowing her voice to fade as a sigh.

"What is?" said Landon anxiously. Would Ravusmane hurry up and get back here already?

Bridget glanced at the hill and then at her brother and sister. "This is." Her voice did that breezy thing again. After she had spoken, it seemed as if it might have been merely the wind. "This hill."

Her eyes darted to the woods and back, and Landon realized what all three of them must be feeling. Without Ravusmane nearby, they felt alone and exposed. Vulnerable. He shifted his eyes about. Who was out in the forest? Were other Arcans roaming the woods? Where was Max? Landon wanted to run and hide. To do something other than stand beside this bare hill and wait.

Wait.

Landon froze. Where was Ravusmane? He'd last dipped into the woods, but then he hadn't come back out again. At least Landon couldn't spot him. Had something happened to Ravusmane? Had an Arcan sliced him with a sword? Or shot him with an arrow? Landon's body felt like stone. Was an entire band of Arcans waiting to ambush them? A breeze blew by. A real one this time, not merely the whispery sound of Bridget's voice. *I see you, Landon Snow,* it seemed to say.

I see you—

Something came from behind the hill.

Landon turned and raised Vates's stick, ready to strike.

It was Ravusmane.

Landon lowered the stick and slumped against it. "Don't *do* that!" he said, speaking louder than he'd intended. He wanted to scream from so much pent-up anxiety. Pressing his lips together, a guttural moaning, growling sound came from Landon. He couldn't help it. He pounded the earth with the stick and growled again.

Ravusmane looked at him. "That was pretty good. You can almost speak animal when you really want to."

Landon flared his eyes at him.

"Sorry about sneaking up on you. I had to slip in the woods and steal back around undetected. It's the only way I could really make sure no one's out there. Or"—he motioned behind the hill—"back there."

"And?" asked Holly quietly but urgently.

Ravusmane nodded reassuringly. "There's no one there."

Landon thought about that breezy voice he thought he'd heard. "Are you sure?"

"No one but us. At least not for a half mile out or so, which will give me just enough time."

"Enough time for what?"

"To get us inside the house and get you three suited up for the mission."

Bridget, Holly, and Landon looked at each other.

"So, this *is* Vates's house?" Landon's rapid heartbeat shifted from apprehension back toward excitement. Still, he wasn't sure how this could be the same house he'd remembered. He was about to ask where the door was when he decided maybe he should *believe* and then he would *see*.

Landon looked at the hillside and tried to believe. He closed his eyes. When he opened them, he didn't see a door and two windows. But he did see a large gray wolf sniff the grass, find a spot, and then begin digging until black dirt was flying like spray behind a speedboat.

Chapter Twelve

Ravusmane had soon dug a tunnel into the hill. His long, gray tail had disappeared inside, while singular clumps of dirt kept ejecting every couple of seconds. Landon wanted to peek in, but he didn't want to get smacked in the face by a dirt clod. So he waited.

"Okay," Ravusmane eventually growled from within. "I'll need someone's help here."

"Can I?" Bridget asked eagerly. She looked directly at her big brother. Landon glanced at Holly, and then he put his head inside the opening.

"What do you need help with? The door?"

"Window," came the reply.

"Oh." Landon looked at Bridget and nodded. "Okay. But be careful." It was one of those statements older people made when they were nervous about something. So they said, "Be careful," as if that might help their nerves as much as the person to whom they told it.

"Yeah," said Holly. "Be careful."

Bridget ducked into the tunnel and disappeared. As Landon listened, he anxiously scanned the tree line. It was eerie standing just outside the forest's edge, barely able to penetrate its shadowy interior. Someone could be in there, anyone, not even a stone's throw away, and Landon wouldn't be able to see him.

He wished Bridget would hurry or that Ravusmane would come back out and do another reconnoitering run. Finally, he heard a muffled bark. Funny, he couldn't tell whether it had been Bridget or Ravusmane.

"Okay! I've got it! Come in!"

Landon bent toward the dark hole, but then he gestured to Holly. "Ladies first." She didn't argue and crawled inside. Landon gave one final look toward the trees, and then something caused him to look up. The sky was hazy, a low mass of shifting grays that could be smoke or fog or clouds. Or all combined. Landon sniffed the air. Faint forest and distant smoke. No animal or human or creature smell that he could detect. He knelt by the hole and slithered inside.

He was partway into the house before he realized he was already crossing the window's threshold. The sill felt flat and rigid beneath his knees, and then he toppled forward. At the same moment, someone lit a match and illuminated a lantern. "No firefly," Landon muttered, thinking of the glowing bugs that had provided the lighting the last time he had visited this place.

The lantern seemed to cast shadows as much as light. It

felt as if they were inside a mine deep within the earth, which, in a sense, they were. It felt so lonely and cold without outside light coming through the windows. Only the faintest of gray twilight spilled from the tunnel. What made the place even more depressing was the state it was in. Books lay open facedown on the floor—a position neither Vates nor Ditty would ever leave them in (and Hardy would not open a book in the first place). Shards of broken earthenware lay strewn about—mugs and plates Landon had once used to drink ginger ale or tea and eat bread, pie, or crumplets from. Cobwebs laced corners and niches, and for a sickening moment, Landon wondered if a firefly or two may have met its fate there. This just wasn't the dusty-yet-bright, warm, cozy place he had remembered. He had been so anxious to get inside, but now he was feeling just as anxious to leave again.

"This is Vates's place?" Holly asked, her tone matching Landon's gloominess.

"It's kinda creepy," Bridget said in a hushed voice, as if the spiders might be listening.

"What happened here?" Landon directed the question to Ravusmane, who was snuffling among the books on a lower shelf along the back wall.

"It was done intentionally, if you mean the ransacked look of the place," said the wolf. "Ah." With his forepaws, which were still black from digging dirt, he pulled down some books, adding more spilled tomes to the floor. Landon flinched at this treatment but didn't say anything.

"Vates did this himself?" he said frowning. It was hard to believe. "But why?"

Ravusmane thrust his head into an opening among the books. A muffled clattering sounded before the remaining books on that shelf came sliding out as one, plopping to the floor. Ravusmane reemerged, carrying in his jaws a wide burlap sack obviously full of heavy objects. The sack fell atop the spilled books, breaking its fall. Landon still heard sharp clinks coming from inside the sack. His eyes widened when he guessed what might be inside.

Ravusmane tugged with his teeth at a cord securing one end of the sack. "Please help," he said backing up. "The knot's fairly tight."

Holly stepped in. "I've got it." Her expression shifted from confident to impatient to downright perturbed as she feverishly worked at the tied binding. "Augh!" She flung out her hands and let the end of the sack droop toward the floor. "My fingers hurt."

Landon was about to give it a try when Bridget moved in, lifted the tied end, picked gently at the rope, and then gasped when it slipped apart in her nimble little fingers.

"Good work, Bridge," said Landon admiringly. Bridget was looking at the rope in her hand as if it had come off by magic. "Thanks," she said distractedly.

"Well, I loosened it for you," said Holly, though she was being more sarcastic than haughty. "What's inside?"

Landon's gut tightened at the question. "Swords," he blurted. "And. . ." He paused, feeling his face twitch despite himself.

"And?" said Ravusmane, glancing up at him. "You already know, don't you?"

Landon sighed. "And armor. Swords and armor. For us."

He looked at his two sisters. They returned his stare, their eyes glistening in the lantern light.

Holly gulped. "I suppose I could have guessed that. I mean, it looks and sounds like it could be, uh, swords." She gulped again and then glanced at the large bundle of burlap. "But you knew, Landon. Didn't you?"

Landon blinked. "Yeah. It was the only time my Bible turned on its own in *my* room—at home. It happened earlier this summer. The night Mom and Dad told us they were going to go on a cruise." He closed his eyes for a moment, remembering the flashing blue light against his window shade, the high-pitched shriek outside (both of which had come from a police car, he discovered), and then the passage he'd found underlined in the final book of the Bible, Revelation:

> *And there was war in heaven: Michael and his angels fought against the dragon; and the dragon fought and his angels, and prevailed not; neither was their place found any more in heaven. And the great dragon was cast out, that old serpent, called the Devil, and Satan, which deceiveth the whole world: he was cast out into the earth, and his angels were cast out with him.*

"The dragon," Landon whispered, although he wasn't sure if he'd muttered aloud or not. His Bible had then flipped to the book of Ephesians, where he'd found these words underlined:

> *Put on the whole armour of God, that ye may be able*

to stand against the wiles of the devil. For we wrestle not against flesh and blood, but against principalities, against powers, against the rulers of the darkness of this world, against spiritual wickedness in high places.

"We need to put on the armor," he said, opening his eyes. "The whole armor. . .of the Auctor."

"And quickly," said Ravusmane. "Before *he* comes."

All three children spoke at once. "Flying Fire?" said Bridget. "Volucer Ignis?" said Holly. "Malus Quidam," said Landon with a shiver.

Ravusmane tilted his head. Then he answered, "Yes. The one with many dark names. Or his minions. We don't want them sniffing around, either."

Landon suddenly felt claustrophobic, as if the underground dwelling might close in or collapse or, even worse, they might be found out and trapped inside by their enemy.

"Can we drag that outside and put it on out there?" He indicated the sack and its contents.

Ravusmane nodded. "Good thinking. Easier to climb back out armorless for you anyway. I'll get in the tunnel first. Deliver the pack to me open end first, and I'll drag it outside for you." Ravusmane climbed into the tunnel and then turned around, facing back into the dwelling. After backing up a few steps, he paused. "Only," he said, switching his head side to side.

"What?" asked Landon. "What is it? Isn't there enough room?"

"No," said Ravusmane. "It's just that this isn't the best

direction for me to come outside. Blind and defenseless."

Landon smirked, picturing the wolf's rear end emerging from the hill. "I'll go first, then," he said. "Make sure the coast is clear."

Ravusmane whimpered a soft complaint, but then he maneuvered to one side to allow Landon to squeeze through next to him. Ravusmane's fur felt luxuriously soft. Landon brushed it with one hand before concentrating on the dirt tunnel before him.

Was it because he had just been inside, or had it actually grown lighter outside? Climbing out from the hole, Landon crouched on the ground next to it, pressing his back to the hill. When he discovered the reason for the increased illumination, his body went rigid as stone.

"Ravus," he whispered hoarsely, his voice tapering to silence out of fear. "Ravus, *hurry!*" It was all Landon could say, and then he merely watched as a column of fire fell from the sky, rippling like a fat bolt of lightning traveling in slow motion. No booming thunder followed—only a high-pitched squeal that made Landon's blood run cold.

Two more streams of flame burst forth like comets zooming toward earth. The final blast appeared closer than the first two. A reddish glow erupted above the treetops. It seemed Landon could even hear the trees crying out in anguish. He feared he might be next. "Ravus—" His voice rasped, barely escaping his clenched throat. "Rav—"

A furry tail and rump appeared beside him. Landon resisted the urge to grab Ravusmane's tail and pull. That probably wouldn't help, he decided. This was the hardest wait of Landon's life—for a backward-moving wolf from a hillside tunnel.

Ravusmane was growling like a dog unwilling to release a blanket. "Err-err-*err!*" His rear paws finally slid down behind him, and he came tumbling out, the burlap bag dropping with a clattery *thud.* Landon reacted instantly, prying open the sack's mouth and reaching in to grab something.

"Ouch!" He yanked his hand back out. Blood dripped from his thumb and forefinger. "The blades are at the open end?" Reflexively he licked his wounds and then grimaced at both the taste and the sting. The slicing pain had at least roused him from his fear. *All right,* he told himself. *Slow down. Remain calm.* That was another thing people said when they were nervous. *Be careful. Remain calm.*

A line of fire lit up the sky.

"Forget that," Landon muttered to himself. Ignoring the throbbing in his fingers, he leaped over the sack and took hold of the bottom end. Like a magician whipping a tablecloth out from under standing dishes, Landon yanked the bag away. A few items spilled out, but something snagged inside. Landon found himself bouncing against the hill with the still mostly full sack.

"Augh!" he howled in frustration.

As the forest hushed to a restive quiet, Landon wished he had held his anxious tongue. For a minute, everything seemed still. Ravusmane's ears began to twitch as he hunted the trees with his eyes. He sniffed the air. Then Landon saw it. Just after he saw it, he could sense it. Something was stirring.

The sky is moving. The clouds are shifting. The smoke is lifting. The very gentlest of breezes filtered the forest.

It's the calm before the storm.

Bridget's dark ringlets emerged, followed closely by Holly's straight blond locks. The girls clambered out, and before either could speak, Ravusmane whispered through gritted teeth, "His ears are keen. He approaches. You need the armor on—*now.*"

His words pierced Landon's fear like a spear, driving home the point of their immediate mission.

Get the armor on.

First, get it out of the bag.

Picturing Bridget's gentle loosening of the knot, Landon carefully and calmly lifted the bag until the swords and pieces of armor fell out on their own.

Be careful. Remain calm. Good pieces of advice, after all.

Somehow, the items even seemed to have arranged themselves for their respective bearers and wearers. "Bridget, you first." Landon called her over and helped her don the smallest set of armor: a breastplate, two shin guards, a belt with short scabbard, and finally a helmet that was a cross between the shell of a bicycle helmet and a colander. The armor was all light, shiny, and strong. Despite its thinness, Landon found he couldn't begin to bend or dent it. Not that he was trying to, of course.

"Okay, Holly. You're next."

A shrieking from the sky sent a shiver along Landon's spine, but he did not waver from his task. Holly first extended her hands, facing up, to Bridget. Across her palms lay a short blade that was more a dagger than a sword. Bridget silently lifted it by its handle and then sheathed it at her side.

After Holly was fully outfitted, Landon handed her a sword that felt light and swift in his hand. She slipped it into her scabbard and proceeded to help him put on his armor. He was beginning to feel like a catcher getting ready to crouch behind home plate, save for the missing facemask. His sword looked familiar, and he soon learned why. Along its handle had been scratched three initials. B.G.B. "Bartholomew G. Benneford," Landon smilingly whispered as he hoisted his sword heavenward, briefly tempting lightning to strike before gliding it into its case with a satisfying ring.

Ravusmane had remained surprisingly quiet throughout this process. Snatching up the empty sack in his mouth, he now sprang into action.

"Come!" he commanded, barking through the burlap.

The children followed as Ravusmane bounded toward the forest. As soon as they entered the dusky cover of the trees, a brilliant glow shot down behind them. Forest shadows rose. Landon glanced back, squinting, as a fireball engulfed Vates's hill. A plume of flame rose and then darted into the tunnel like a snake. Landon felt the air sucked from his lungs a moment before the hill exploded.

Chapter Thirteen

Heat! Light! Noise!

Hot! Bright! Loud!

It seemed Landon had been separated from reality and thrown into chaos. For a long, terrifying moment, he was alone, thrown down by a blast of fire, enveloped by a boom of thunder. He was covering his ears, but the sound was too big. Painful. His ears throbbed. It buffeted his head. The next thing he knew, the light and heat and noise were gone. And then came the rain.

Real rain—water—would have been nice. Refreshing and cool. This rain was depressing. Falling from the colorless sky came clods of dirt, shards of pottery, slivers of wood, splinters of glass, and saddest of all: charred pages of books. It was like a plane had flown overhead, dumping leaflets. For several minutes, the paper kept falling. Some pieces became impaled among the tree branches. Some fluttered all the way to earth. One torn piece floated right to Landon, and he caught it in his palm like a strange white leaf. It was blank. But when he turned it over he found these handwritten words:

> *Could it be chance, mere circumstance*
> *The man eats cow eats grass eats. . .*

And there the paper was torn off.

"*Soil*," said Landon, completing the phrase. "*And then man dies, and when he lies, to soil he does return?*"

A high-pitched shriek pricked the hair on Landon's neck. He shivered and looked toward the sky. The hazy fog had shifted. The beast sounded far away. As the paper with the opening of the Auctor's Riddle fell from his hand and drifted to earth, Landon muttered, "I hate that dragon."

It felt right to hate this time. But it didn't feel good. It did not feel good in Landon's heart at all. Nothing about this evil dragon could evoke any goodness in anything.

"Landon?" Bridget was whimpering. "What happened? I want to go home."

Holly was staring at the hill, or what was left of it. Flames continued to lick from behind a crude ridge along where Landon guessed the door and windows—the front wall—had been. The place was gutted. Vates's hill and home were gone.

"His books," Landon whispered, gazing numbly at the pages spread between the wood and the remains of the hill. A few pages were burning, blackening, curling, and disappearing. Smoke stung Landon's eyes. He suddenly had to choke back a sob.

Hatred again rocked his stomach. He thought he might be sick.

"I'm going to kill him," he muttered through clenched teeth. "I'm going to kill him." Unsheathing his sword, he raised it high, then plunged it into the earth with a scream.

Bridget was crying.

"Landon, don't. You're scaring her more." Holly's voice trembled, but beneath it she sounded remarkably calm.

Landon wanted to sink his sword into the ground again and again, piercing the dragon's hide with each blow. But Holly was right. Squeezing the hilt tightly till it hurt, he slid the blade back inside its sheath. Landon was heaving with emotion and frustration. Vates's house had been like home to him, too. Bridget and Holly had never seen it before, so they were blessedly spared some of the pain from seeing it destroyed.

"I'm sorry," Landon said, staying a tremor in his sword-bearing hand. "It's just that I hate him and I want to kill him."

"Yeah," said Holly, sounding more herself. "We could see that. Point well taken."

Bridget still cried. Landon looked at her and sighed. When he went to her, she flinched warily at first but then melted into her big brother's arms, where her cries softened into wavering breaths and sniffles.

Landon held her tight. Their armor clicked between them, but neither seemed to notice the bulk or strangeness of it. It added to their comfort, in fact.

"Where's Ravusmane?"

Holly's question startled him. Even Bridget held her breath. Brother and sister let each other go. The smoke was clearing.

Dust settling. If only those shifting clouds would go away—or drop some rain first and then depart for cheery blue skies.

Bridget sniffled one last time. "Is he. . .gone?"

"Maybe he had to scare away more Arcans," offered Landon. But then he wished he hadn't, as the thought of Arcans only added to his anxiety.

"It's me, it's me," came Ravusmane's voice, just ahead of his bounding presence. "Didn't mean to abandon you. Only reconnoitering the path ahead. We need to move on. He's coming back."

"The dragon?" Landon resisted the urge to unsheathe his sword.

Ravusmane growled in the affirmative.

Holly turned back to the remnants of Vates's place. "But what's left to burn? The hill is demolished."

"He likes to play the billows," said Ravusmane mysteriously. "Come!"

This wasn't the time for more questions. Landon had no desire to witness another explosion or blast of fire. As he and his sisters took off at a quick trot behind the wolf, who was obviously dragging his pace so they could keep up, Landon imagined staying behind and planting himself high in a tree. Then maybe, if the dragon flew down low enough, his sword could find its mark. "Be true," Landon muttered as he patted the hilt. "When the time comes, be true."

"Who are you talking to?" Holly asked over her huffing.

"My sword," Landon said.

"Oh."

It was amazing how far debris from the blast had dropped. A bit of a mug or plate here. A black iron latch from a door there. And still pages—thousands of pages from those precious, ancient books. Landon wondered if Holly was counting them. It would be hard for her not to—at least the sheets she was stepping on. Landon tried to leap over as many as he could out of respect for the printed page. But for a while, they were hard to avoid; the ground coverage was too dense.

Ravusmane veered to the right and then back to the left around a tight copse of trunks. The children followed. Landon's lungs were beginning to burn, but neither Holly nor Bridget had yet complained, so he wasn't about to, either. He wondered if he was the only one who wanted to seek revenge, who was so enraged by this act of blatant, mindless destruction. Maybe the girls were being powered more by pure fear. A good dose of fear can fire up the adrenal glands. That was for sure.

Fire up. Landon almost smiled at the pun, despite himself. A glance through the treetops toward the sky revealed nothing to him about the whereabouts of Flying Fire. *Volucer Ignis.* The dragon. The beast. The wicked creature he wanted to kill. What had Ravusmane said? The dragon liked to "play the billows"? As if in answer to this thought, Landon heard a screeching howl. It hadn't come from overhead. The hair-raising sound had been directed at them seemingly from behind. Before Landon could turn his head to look, he felt the wind. A powerful gust of air at his back, propelling him forward.

"Whoa!" he shouted, feeling like a reenergized sprinter. "This will help move us quicker!"

Ravusmane glanced back, his eyes flared in dread. "Quickly!" He faced forward and plunged ahead, compelling the kids to keep up with him.

Holly started speaking. "We're going as fast as we—aaaahhhh!" Her scream started when Ravusmane suddenly vanished before their eyes. Then all three of them screamed when the earth gave way beneath them and they plummeted into a deep, dark pit.

"It's all right," Ravusmane was saying as soon as they landed in the darkness. His furry presence was right there, and he did help to calm and quiet them. "I didn't have time to explain—or warn you—earlier. It's good we're down here. I forgot this one was here myself."

"This is *good*?" said Landon. They must be at least ten feet below ground. "But why—"

A powerful wind rushed overhead, drowning out other sounds. In the pit, they felt only a gentle stirring of air, and already Landon was a little happier about being down here. The wind did not let up. It only picked up. And then came the fire.

The only experience Landon could compare it to was seeing a TV show where an iron door opened on a huge furnace. Inside appeared a wavering wall of fire. He didn't remember what the show was about, only that one image returned as he stared at a much larger wall of fire blazing past overhead. He closed his eyes and ducked, covering his face now from the brightness and the heat. Soon he felt as if he were melting. When the flames finally ceased, Landon found he was soaked with sweat.

"Is everyone all right?"

It was Ravusmane.

Bridget whimpered.

Holly coughed and wheezed.

Dust was pouring over them, burnt remains of paper and leaves.

"That was playing?" Landon's eyes felt itchy and irritated, though he dared not rub them. "Playing the—what did you say?" His voice was hoarse. He was thirsty.

"Playing the billows," said Ravusmane. "Fanning his own flames with his wings."

"Well, if that's playing," said Holly roughly, "I'd hate to see what he's like when he's serious."

Ravusmane's silence spoke all too loudly.

"I want to go home," said Bridget.

Landon hesitated before lightly and swiftly touching the hilt of his sword. He drew his hand away expecting it to be hot. But it was not. Same for the rest of his armor. Though he was sweating beneath it all, he realized the light, cool steel had thwarted much of the intense heat from his body. Poor Ravusmane, he thought, with all that fur and no armor.

Landon sighed. "Let's pray that we get home, Bridge, after we help set the valley people free from this wretched beast. Okay?"

" 'Wretched beast'?" Holly smiled mockingly.

Landon shrugged. "That's what he is. Wretched. Beast."

Bridget had bowed her head and folded her hands. Landon and Holly glanced at each other and did the same. Even Ravusmane lowered his head. After asking the Auctor for strength and help and a safe return home, and thanking Him for this protective pit, the children said, "Amen."

Ravusmane then growled deeply and respectfully before saying, "To the Auctor's will."

Landon felt like hoisting a mug. "The Auctor's will!"

"I think it's his will that we get out of this hole now," Bridget offered.

"Our swords," said Landon, thinking quickly. He stood, glancing warily for flames or beating wings.

"He's gone. . .for now," said Ravusmane.

Landon then plunged his sword into the dirt wall about waist high. "Yours next, Holly." She unsheathed her sword and handed it to him. "And Bridget?"

"Mine's just a little knife," she muttered.

"Which is why it's a perfect crampon to help me climb out," said Landon extending his hand.

"Cramp what?" Bridget wrinkled her brow.

Landon laughed. "A pick, like for mountain climbing."

"Oh." She handed it to him.

And Landon handed it to Holly. "You first. I'll go last. Up you go."

"Sure," said Holly. "Send the pretty maiden to meet the dragon." She placed the back of her hand to her forehead. "Fare thee well, brave knight."

Landon rolled his eyes. "Get out of here, Holly."

She stepped onto the hilt of Landon's sword, then onto her own, and reaching as far as she could over the edge, she plunged Bridget's dagger into the earth and pulled herself out.

"Good work, Holly!" Landon didn't yell too loudly, just in case.

Holly's head appeared in the gray light overhead. "How are Bridget and Ravusmane going to make it?"

"I'll help Bridget," said Landon. He glanced at the wolf, a little sad and embarrassed. "Uh. . ."

"I'll need your help, too, if you don't mind. But not like Bridget." Ravusmane bared his teeth in something like a smile. "I haven't survived the burning forest on my good looks, you know."

Landon nodded stupidly. "Burning forest?"

Ravusmane's smile withered. "What used to be Wonderwood, our home. It's now the dragon's playground. A smoldering forest."

Landon sighed. Then he frowned. "So even if we can get the people—"

"And animals," Bridget added.

"And animals away from Volucer Ignis, where will we go? I hadn't thought of that." The mission suddenly seemed more hopeless than ever, despite their prayer for the Auctor's help. What was the point of a rescue if there was nowhere to go?

"I don't know." Ravusmane appeared neither saddened nor ruffled by this problem. "We'll trust the Auctor to provide a way, and a where—"

"Hellooo down there! We'll trust for the way and the where, but I think you should get out of the pit *now*."

Landon glanced up. "Something wrong?"

In a quieter voice, Holly said, "We may have company."

Landon hesitated only a moment. "Bridge, let's go." He helped her step onto the first sword, and then he pushed her other foot higher so she could reach Holly's sword. Meanwhile

Holly stretched down as far as she could until she reached Bridget's hand. Scraping and kicking down clods of dirt, Bridget scrambled her way up and out, holding on to her sister.

"If you'll crouch down here like me," Ravusmane instructed, "I'll use your back for leverage."

By the time Landon was down on all fours, Ravusmane was circling the pit like a mad dog. Suddenly, he jumped onto Landon's back—"Oof!"—and then leaped from the pit as if launched by a springboard. The girls cheered.

Landon removed his sword from the wall, where it had been loosened from his sisters' climbs, and sheathed it. Jamming his foot where the sword had been, he reached Holly's sword and climbed out.

"My sword," said Holly.

"Right," Landon said. "Bridget, can you help me?"

Bridget frowned. Then she nodded, her face showing recognition. She lay on the ground, looking into the pit. Landon knelt behind her, took hold of her ankles, and slowly lowered her down the hole. When he heard, "Got it!" he carefully drew her back out.

"Company, you say?" Landon glanced at Holly as he brushed off his knees. It seemed a silly thing to do, the brushing, as they were all quite filthy with dust and dirt. He wasn't surprised to notice Ravusmane was absent. Knowing the wolf was reconnoitering the path ahead brought comfort this time rather than fear.

"Not the dragon—that wretched beast," said Holly with a smirk. "But others."

"Which way do we go?" said Bridget.

A resounding "Woof!" answered the question, and Landon led his sisters deeper into the forest. Their next stop would be at the river.

Chapter Fourteen

On the way to the river, Ravusmane led the children widely around two fires. He paused briefly to point out a pit on either side, where they could have dived had Volucer Ignis decided to play any more billows behind them. Thankfully, the wretched dragon failed to appear.

The sight of flowing water in the midst of such a dry and dusty forest was a welcome view indeed. Ravusmane stopped atop the bank, looked—and sniffed—to his left and to his right, and then plunged into the tall grass along the slope. "Here!" he barked.

With Vates's staff, Landon parted the grass to find a stockpile of stones. Holly and Bridget peered in. "These are the stones that turn into lily pads on the river?" asked Holly, her expression both curious and excited.

Landon nodded. "Far as I know, any stone will in this river. Come on."

"I'll take the stick," said Ravusmane, clamping his jaws gently on the staff. As soon as Landon let go, the four-foot staff shrank to a stick about a foot long. Ravusmane looked up, and for a moment Landon wondered if the wolf wanted to play fetch. Through clenched teeth, Ravusmane suggested the children use their helmets to hold the stones.

"Good thinking," said Landon.

When he and Holly and Bridget had filled their helmets, they formed a line along the river's edge. It was decided that Bridget would throw first and lead the way, followed by Holly and then Landon and Ravusmane. After two test throws to see if it was really true, Bridget took a deep breath. "Ready?" she asked, her voice quavering with excitement.

"Ready."

"Okay."

"Okay."

"We're ready, Bridge. Right behind you."

"Yeah. Okay."

"Do you want me to go first?" asked Holly.

Bridget nodded.

The girls switched places, and Holly bowed her head briefly. Looking up, she resembled a track star about to begin a race. "Go!" she said, following her own command with a throw, waiting for the rock to strike the water, and then jumping from shore to the lily-pad-shaped stone spreading on the surface.

"Go! Go!" Landon and Bridget were both hopping and shouting. "Okay! Okay!" Bridget made it safely to the stone, and Landon saw it already beginning to shrink as he leaped onto it.

Ravusmane landed alongside him, not behind, which startled Landon but then urged him on. "Let's go! Let's go!" he kept shouting.

The river was wide. Landon realized when they were about twenty-five yards out that he'd ridden on horseback on Melech the previous times he'd crossed it. Holly ran out of stones well before the halfway mark.

"We have to jump farther," Landon said between breaths. "Farther! Go, Bridget. Throw! Throw!"

Bridget glanced sideways in response and then charged to take the lead. She looked like a scared rabbit. When a rabbit is scared, it will either freeze like a statue or bolt like lightning. Fortunately, Bridget was employing the latter response. Landon almost laughed as it took everything he had to keep up. Twice his foot touched down and pushed him forward just ahead of the diminishing edge of stone. He was running on pure adrenaline now, as surely his sisters were, as well.

They were just over halfway across when Landon slipped and fell. His helmet bounced, scattering stones ahead of them, and then it bounced again before rolling along the extra pads that had popped up from the spilled stones. Bridget had enough runway to stop and then retreat as Landon's helmet bounced past her. The children and Ravusmane stood in silent shock as the extended platform began shrinking beneath them. Landon's helmet rode the rock back in, wobbling but not falling into the water.

"Take the stick," Ravusmane commanded. Landon grabbed it without thinking, and the stick became a full-length staff. "Your helmet, too."

Landon stooped and snatched it up. The foursome couldn't collapse into a tighter group. Soon they only saw their feet beneath them, and then they went in.

"Grab the stick!" said Ravusmane.

Landon swallowed a mouthful of water. "I already—*glub*—did!"

"Everyone!" said Ravusmane. He dipped his snout and came up pushing Bridget toward the stick. "Grab it and hold on!"

Landon quickly understood two things. One, the armor he and his sisters wore was buoyant. *It floated.* None of them was sinking. Two, Ravusmane meant to propel them all to shore as they held on to the staff: Landon on one side, his sisters grasping the other, and Ravusmane biting the middle and doing a powerful doggy paddle. Landon and Holly helped with some scissor kicks.

After climbing ashore and catching their breath, Holly said, "Well, thanks a lot, Landon."

"I'm sorry. I didn't mean to—"

Holly was shaking her head. "I don't mean *that.* I mean thanks for making me lose count of the stones we were throwing. I figured it could come in handy to know exactly how many are needed to make it across, in case we ever have to do that again." She glared at him but then smiled.

"Oh. Yeah. That is a good idea. Well, did you get a count until I fell?"

Holly sighed. "Of course I did. But believe it or not, I don't remember if it was 27, 36, or 45. Or maybe 54. It was a multiple of nine, that much I know."

"We'll just have to ballpark it," said Landon.

"Shh!" said Bridget suddenly. "He's listening."

Ravusmane had climbed the bank and was scanning the terrain in either direction, his ears pointing forward like radar. He turned and came back down.

"The animals are out," he said plainly. But he didn't sound happy.

"They're outside the wall? How did they—?"

"They didn't escape," said Ravusmane harshly. "The Arcans let them out." He turned his head strangely and loudly sniffed. It was the most emotion Landon had yet detected in the wolf's behavior.

"Why?" said Bridget. She had shuffled closer and was stroking Ravusmane's furry neck.

The wolf looked up. "For sport."

Just then, a spine-tingling cry came from the forest—the pitiful scream of an animal in anguish. Landon bowed his head, squeezing the hilt of his sword with one hand and Vates's staff with the other. Bridget trembled and cried, and Holly hugged her and covered her hand that now clutched Ravusmane's fur. The wolf stood stock-still.

Another chilling sound followed, and it was just as strange. But the effect was entirely different. It sounded like laughter. Mocking, scornful, evil laughter. It seemed to mock laughter itself, this eerie howling that carried no life or happiness or humor, only wickedness and violence and death.

"There will be more Arcans about," said Ravusmane coolly. He seemed extra detached but no less focused. "Which may work to our advantage."

Landon frowned. "Our advantage?"

Holly looked from Ravusmane to Landon. Bridget was catching her breath in hiccups.

Turning his head slightly, Ravusmane continued. "We need to get to the Stepping Stone unseen. From there we may proceed even more quickly—in full view—all the way to the wall."

"What?" said Holly.

"Wha–hut?" Bridget sniffed.

Another animal scream punctured the air. Before the mocking laughter could reach them, Ravusmane decided to move.

"Come. Hurry. They're distracted. I'll explain at the stone."

Landon looked at his sisters, and they looked at him. What choice did they have? After Ravusmane performed another forest check from his perch atop the bank, they all clambered over and made a beeline for the trees.

The Stepping Stone looked older than Landon had remembered. The three rock tiers ascending against the tree trunk were cracked and crumbling, as if the whole thing might collapse if he sat on it. The sight made him feel sad.

"Strike the stone with the staff," said Ravusmane.

Landon was hoping for an explanation first, but he raised the staff and brought it down—*whack*—upon the stone. Sure enough, its cracks widened and it crumpled before their eyes. Ravusmane pawed at the rubble, soon unearthing three quivers full of arrows along with three bows. And then he dug out three animal skulls.

"You are now hunting me," said Ravusmane. He turned to

Landon and then Holly and finally Bridget, whom he held for a long moment with his gaze. To Landon's surprise, Bridget slowly began to nod. Still, her eyes kept darting to the skulls.

"Okay," she said, "as long as we miss, right?" She even smiled, and Ravusmane's expression softened, as well.

"That would be appreciated, little miss."

"And big miss," said Holly. "I think I understand. We're 'hunting you' as we run to the wall?"

Ravusmane nodded. "Only do not engage any Arcan. Do not even glance their way. As long as you are intent on pursuing me, they will take no notice of us."

"They won't shoot at you, too, will they, Ravusmane? If we're already chasing you?" Landon's chest hurt just thinking about it.

Ravusmane didn't waver. "Do not engage the Arcans even then. Do not look at them. If I should fall, you must run to the wall. Locate a shape like the Stepping Stone along the base. Well,"—he pawed at the heap of stones—"a shape as this stone was when we found it, and in the rock you will find a round notch. Insert the staff and push, and the stone should yield."

Landon's throat and mouth felt dry, though his palms were growing moist. Numbly, he handed a quiver and bow to each of his sisters, and then he slung the third over his back. Next they fitted an animal skull atop each helmet. Bridget put on a brave face, although she and Holly both looked about as glum as Landon was feeling. They certainly didn't appear to be three hunters eager to pursue their prey.

Ravusmane seemed to read their collective mood. "They haven't shot me yet." He made his wolfy smirk. "You will need to be more convincing than this. You must pretend you're having fun. You must look like you want to strike me down, like nothing would give you more nasty pleasure."

Landon kicked at a remaining hunk of the Stepping Stone, reducing it to rubble. Holly swung her bow miserably. Bridget hiccupped back more tears.

Ravusmane sighed. "Listen. I'm not an easy target. And when we're on the run, don't you worry about hitting me. Only take care not to trip"—he glanced at Landon—"or accidentally hit one another. Nothing worse than friendly fire. Shoot an arrow into the trees every so often to make a good show of it. Listen," he repeated, "the sooner we reach the wall—*together*—the sooner we get to see Vates and Melech and Hardy—"

"And the bears? And Epops?" said Bridget, perking up.

Ravusmane looked at her and hesitated, but only for a moment. "And the bears, of course. Epops—oh yes."

"Ditty?" said Landon. "And her parents?"

"Yes, yes. All of your old friends. They will be so happy to see you." But Ravusmane didn't sound entirely happy.

"What about Ludo?" said Holly. "How is he doing?" Ravusmane seemed to be getting impatient while Landon had to admit he didn't mind stalling some more, despite the hope of seeing his friends again.

Ravusmane paused. "Ludo." He turned his head slightly and tilted it. "Ludo has grown weak. He's a susceptible fellow, he is."

"Susceptible to what?" said Landon. He had a very uneasy feeling in his stomach.

A cry pierced the air, drowned promptly by raucous howls

and whoops. Ravusmane snapped to attention. "We have no more time. Give chase!" And he bounded off through the trees.

"Oh, dear," said Holly, staring after the gray blur.

"Don't lose him!" said Landon, feeling his heart jolt into high gear. Upon taking a step, however, a sharp *twang* stopped him cold. There was Bridget grasping her bow with its string still quivering.

"I think I hit a leaf," she said.

Landon laughed, and then they all three laughed—sounding as wicked and mean as they could—as they raced into the woods after Ravusmane.

The chase continued. Sometimes Ravusmane let the children get close, and then he would quickly bound ahead again. His bouncing gray tail led them right to the wall. From what first appeared beyond the trees as a distant stone fence, the wall rapidly grew monstrous. If it had been smooth and curved inward, it might have been a dam. A massive dam in the middle of the forest. It was certainly taller and perhaps just as wide as the Great Wall of China.

Ravusmane halted at the foot of the wall. The chase was over. They had made it.

"Incredible," Holly said, panting and lowering her bow. "Look at all of the stones! It would take me years to count them."

"What's more incredible is the amount of work it must have taken to build this thing." Staring up along the wall made Landon dizzy. To his left, the wall curved outward into the woods. It was the base of a giant turret, giant both in girth and in height. A realization hit Landon like a punch to the gut.

"That's Ludo's tree," he muttered. "So the other towers I'd seen from a distance. . .they must be the Whump Trees. They've built towers around the tallest trees."

"They've built right *onto* the trees, yes," said Ravusmane. "Inside the wall's base are also tree trunks, trees skinned of branches and leaves and then left as part of the bottom infrastructure."

Landon had never thought of a tree being "skinned" before.

"The main entry is through there." Ravusmane indicated the huge column. "Two tall, wood doors out front, where the Arcans pass. We need to find the secret shape." As he set off sniffing along the wall, an animal cried from the forest behind them. Wicked laughter followed and then quickly subsided.

"It sounds like they're coming back already," Landon said.

Holly was watching Ravusmane. "I thought he said to *look* for the secret shape. Why's he sniffing for something and not looking?"

"Well we'd better look then and try to help," said Landon. He glanced at Bridget. "You all right, Bridge?" She nodded, though not too convincingly.

"Here!" Ravusmane called. "Bring the staff."

Bridget kept glancing toward the woods as they hurried to Ravusmane. "It's okay, Bridget," said Landon. "We'll get inside before the Arcans get here."

"But what about the other animals?" she said. "Will they come back, too?"

"Well," said Landon, "I suppose they'll—"

Ravusmane interrupted. "Volucer Ignis," he said quietly.

"He'll hunt them down and finish them off. A hawk swooping on helpless field mice."

The children stood in silence. Finally, Landon spoke softly. "The fires."

Ravusmane sighed. "The spot fires. He can pick them off with fireballs. For some of the larger animals, he likes to use a little more heat."

Holly changed the subject. "Ravusmane, why were you sniffing when you told us to *look* for the shape? Does it have a smell?"

Ravusmane's ears perked up. "Do you really want to know?" he teased.

Holly checked Bridget and then Landon. She shrugged. "Yeah."

Ravusmane stood along the wall and lifted his hind leg toward it.

"Oh," said Holly turning away. "Okay. That's gross."

Ravusmane lowered his leg. "It's how we mark our territory. Perfectly natural. And the nose is much keener than the eye."

"Eww." Bridget pinched her nose. "I'm glad *I* wasn't sniffing."

"All right," said Landon, stooping over to find the round notch in the stone. "Let's get inside this place." He positioned the staff and was about to push, when a voice shouted from above.

"Hey, doggy! I saw that! No peeing on the wall! Come here so I can shoot you!"

Landon froze. He recognized the voice all too well. With his heart beating madly, he spoke through gritted teeth. "Holly, Bridget, keep facing the wall. Do not look up. When I get this open, you go in first."

From the corner of his eye, Landon could see Ravusmane's twitching nose and ears. His tail curled under him.

"I must go draw him off. Don't let him see you go in this door!" Ravusmane commanded.

Before Landon could respond, the wolf bounded into the wood. Landon grabbed Bridget's arm and pulled her close. "Don't watch him go, and don't scream," he whispered urgently. "He doesn't know it's us."

"Who?" whimpered Bridget.

Landon lowered his voice. "Max."

Chapter Fifteen

While Landon, Bridget, and Holly remained frozen, facing the wall, something rustled the leaves of the tree overhead. Then it stopped.

"What are you three doing, anyway?" asked Max. "Why didn't you kill that mongrel while you had the chance?"

Landon and his sisters stayed quiet, breathless, though Landon was tempted to try his bow and arrow again, aiming for a hit this time.

"Can you hear me? Stupid Arcans! Does your branch leader know you're here? Hey! And where did you get that shiny armor?"

Ravusmane howled and yipped, sounding as if he'd been tripped or wounded. Landon's heart clenched inside his chest. Rustling came again from overhead, followed by a *thud* and then running footsteps. Max's voice trailed away. "Gonna get you, doggy! Whoo-hee!"

Landon took a moment to study Bridget's face. "We can't go after him," he said calmly. "Ravusmane wants us to get inside."

Bridget's lower lip quivered. "I know. Let's go."

Landon jammed the staff so hard into the stone it almost splintered. His adrenaline was still flowing, and his nerves were frayed. The stone slid back into darkness, revealing an opening just large enough for them to climb through one at a time. Landon waved Holly in, and when her feet disappeared, he motioned for Bridget to enter. Unable to resist, he took one final look at the forest. He raised Vates's staff in a salute, muttered good-bye, and then turned and lay on his belly to slither into the hole, propelling the staff before him. Landon had the sad feeling that may have been his final glimpse of Wonderwood.

"Ow. Hey. Careful," Holly whispered sharply.

"Sorry," Bridget said. "How far does this go? Landon?"

"I'm right here."

A scraping noise filled the darkness, and then it became totally, solidly black as the secret stone shut behind them.

"I wish we knew where we're going," said Holly.

"Just keep crawling," said Landon. "This must come out somewhere. Hey—" A thought struck him. "If that was Ludo's tree where the big turret was, then this should be the Echoing Green." This realization excited him only briefly, as the deeper they crawled, the more he knew the green could be nothing like it was before, which was simply a great circular clearing of grass in the midst of a ring of trees.

"I feel a draft," said Holly. "Ow. Oh!"

"I didn't touch you," said Bridget.

"I think I found a step. Yes. And it goes down here, to the right. Hey, there's a little light down there. Well, it's not really light; it's only kind of gray, which is better than this pitch-black darkness."

"There are steps?" asked Landon, wondering how they might descend them crawling and wearing armor. Thankfully, they wouldn't have to.

"I can stand up," said Holly. "Here, Bridget." A series of scuffling sounds followed. Landon reached the step, angled right, vaguely saw his sisters though they stood just a few steps down, and slowly arose with his hand stretched overhead as an antenna.

At the bottom of the stairway was a door, which Holly carefully eased open. A clattering of noise filled the passageway, and Holly yanked the door shut. It was quiet. Even in the dim light, Landon could make out the whites of his sisters' eyes.

"What in the world was *that*?"

Landon could only shake his head. "Maybe we should have our swords at the ready," he said, "just in case."

Collectively taking a deep breath, they withdrew their blades. Landon maneuvered to the front and gently pushed on the door. Thrusting out his sword, he lunged into the room. The clattering came from still farther out and was echoing—which made it worse—within this mostly bare room. Rather than shouting over the din, Landon glanced back and motioned with his sword for his sisters to follow. They passed through another doorway into another room, where the noise was still louder. It sounded like hammering, picking, pounding, chiseling. Sort of like how Landon imagined a blacksmith's shop would sound, but with a hundred smithies banging at once.

Enough of this, Landon thought. He sheathed his sword and plugged his ears. This second room had some crude bunks in it, as well as two tables and four chairs. *Odd.* A thin board served as a door to the next room, which was actually a space composed of only three walls. The area directly opposite them, where a fourth wall should be, was open save for some wooden poles or supports. Beyond the poles yawned a cavernous, roughly tiered pit of stone.

Forgetting the noise for a moment, which somehow seemed less intense in this vast open space, Landon, Holly, and Bridget stood at the edge to see hundreds of people across and to either side and deep down in the pit chipping, cutting, loading, hauling, and hoisting pieces of stone. The work went on and on. The sight was so foreign Landon wondered if he was watching insects—ants or bees, perhaps. They appeared oblivious to all but the work at hand.

Amid the clanking cacophony, another sound caught Landon's ear. As he cast his gaze downward toward the spiraling depths, rock dust tickled his nose, and he sneezed. The industry continued unabated, to his relief, except for one figure about three tiers down and to the right. It was a stocky man in drab coveralls holding a pick. Despite the dust and the distance, Landon knew he'd been recognized. And he was glad.

"Hardy," he said, his voice lost to the noise. Nudging Holly and pointing, he repeated more loudly. "Look! It's Hardy!"

But their old friend didn't move from his post. Rather, he turned back around and resumed his chipping. Landon was stunned. Had they come all this way and snuck inside, only to go unrecognized by the people they were hoping to help? It was frustrating, too, being rattled by so much noise. He wanted to at least talk with Holly, but it was impossible. Then he noticed something.

Though Hardy remained busy at work, he was wielding the pick now with only one hand. His other hand was withdrawing something from a pocket. Something like a handkerchief. As Hardy waved the cloth behind him like a tail, Landon sensed it was some kind of signal. A sign, at least, that Hardy recognized him and knew he was there. Then Hardy dropped the cloth, and it sailed down and down, drawing Landon's eyes to a dark figure at the very bottom of the pit. Landon squinted, and his heart leaped inside his chest. Smiling, he now knew what that other noise had been. The neighing of a horse. It was Melech.

A warm breeze blew into the quarry, followed by a screeching cry. Landon glanced up in time to see a black, winged creature pass through the air. The sight of it chilled his blood and tightened every pore in his skin. Though the wind was warm—almost hot—Landon shivered.

When the dragon was gone, everything inside the rock pit changed. The workers dropped their tools where they were and began climbing the circular tiers toward the top. The subsequent quiet was deafening. Landon's ears continued to burn and ring. The dragon's scream had been the horn marking the end of the workday, apparently. It was one of the strangest things Landon had ever seen.

One worker wasn't going with the crowd. He was scaling the

wall like a mountain climber, heading their way. Way down at the tail end of the marching corkscrew of workers was Melech, slowly making his way up.

"Landon and de little misses!" Hardy peered at them over the ledge before clambering onto the floor. He sized up Holly and Bridget. "Or not so little anymore, eh?" He suddenly bowed his head, staring at the floor. "Forgive my looks, if you please. Dey took my hat and all my finery."

Landon laughed, grabbing Hardy's shoulder. "Finery? Since when did you ever dress in finery?"

Hardy winked at him, and Landon knew he had his old friend back. Then Hardy's expression shifted, and he looked thoughtfully at the three children. Suddenly, he spun toward the pit. Stooping over, he called out in a loud yet furtive voice, "Hedgelog! Pitterpat! Songsparrow! Up here!" Hardy motioned vigorously.

A few moments later, three other workers emerged from below, appearing quite bewildered by Hardy's behavior and then even more so at the appearance of Landon, Holly, and Bridget. "Come, come!" Hardy urged. "Time is short before de countdown."

Hardy made the introductions as the two parties stared at one another. And then Hardy shocked them all.

"Off wid de clodes. Swap for swap." He crossed his arms back and forth. "You"—he pointed to Hedgelog, the biggest of the workers, and then at Landon—"and you." He did the same to match Pitterpat with Holly, and then Songsparrow—who was quite small yet strong-looking—with Bridget.

The three blinking workers and Landon and his sisters only

continued gaping at one another.

"Not *all* de clodes," Hardy explained as if it should have been obvious. "Armor for mining suits. Not what's under*nead* de armor and mining suits." He grinned, shaking and rubbing his head. Glancing out at the pit, he resumed crossing his arms. "Fast now. Hurry, hurry! Swords and head helmets, too."

Landon looked at his sisters. "I'm not sure what he has in mind exactly, but of course I trust him. We should do as he says."

Holly agreed, and so they undid their armor piece by piece and laid it on the chalky floor.

The three workers hesitated. Finally, Pitterpat spoke up. "Are these. . .*them*?" He waved his open hand across at Landon and his sisters. "From the outer realm?"

"Aye," said Hardy, settling down for an instant. "Dey've come back—again."

Landon's chest and stomach fluttered. He had a feeling their presence here was about to become more involved. "The outer realm?" He glanced at Hardy.

"From outside of here," said Hardy. "Where you say you come from, again?"

"Button Up," said Landon, not bothering to explain they actually lived in Minneapolis, which was another city in the state of Minnesota, and so on.

"Ah," said Hardy, as if Landon had just said they came from Jupiter.

"Ah," chorused the three workers. "But Tin Nup."

Bridget giggled.

Hardy clapped, and the workers stripped off their coveralls, revealing plain, filthy underclothes that reminded Landon of long underwear. Hedgelog's work garment was heavier than Landon expected and felt like coarse denim. It also reeked of sweat.

"Okay," said Holly, "I was still feeling pretty clean from our dip in the river." She looked meaningfully at Landon. "And I don't really want to slip *this* thing on."

Meanwhile Bridget was already climbing into Songsparrow's suit, and then she handed him her helmet. Landon and Holly looked at each other, shrugged, inhaled deeply, and then held their breath as they donned the coveralls.

"You dree"—Hardy pointed at the workers-turned-warriors—"in dere. And stay put until we come back. Okay?"

Hardy obviously carried some authoritative weight here, even though Hedgelog appeared to outweigh him physically. Pitterpat and Songsparrow joined Hedgelog's nodding.

"Are you. . .they. . .going to fight. . ." Pitterpat gulped. "Him?"

Hardy's eyes narrowed, glinting from his grimy face. "Not yet. I take dem on a tour now, get de lay of de land. Den we come back out fighting." He smiled, which made Landon nervous, and then he rapped Pitterpat's breastplate, causing the startled fellow to flinch. "Fighting wid de armor back on and de swords." Hardy gave Landon and Holly an assuring look before commanding the workers to the back room. They turned and marched away, but not without looking back several times in the process.

"What about this?" Landon raised Vates's staff.

Hardy eyed it up and down, momentarily seeming to drift to another place. His eyes refocused and shifted toward Landon. "Bring it. Bring it," he repeated with a nod. "Now off we go to catch de line. Oh!" His eyes widened. "You are too clean. Stick out like a sour plumb!" He commenced scooping dirt and grit from the floor and wiping it on Landon's face.

"Ow. Hey." Landon grimaced. "I'll do it. Come on," he told his sisters. As they mussed up their hair and coated their faces and other bare skin with dust, Landon thought about movie stars putting on "distressed clothing" and dirt for a role in a movie. He'd heard the clothes were actually brand-new, but they were ripped and soiled to look worn and dirty before being worn by the actors. He bet those clothes didn't smell as grubby as they looked.

"Good enough," said Hardy. "Let's go." He indicated they were to climb back down to a jutting ledge below, from where they could trace the rim of the quarry to catch the end of the line of workers still spiraling their way up toward the surface.

Holly studied her appearance and her brother's and sister's. "But we still don't look like them. Won't we still stand out?"

Hardy shrugged and gave her a strange look. "De Arcans don't really see us. Dey don't really *look*, you know? But dey count. As long as dere's de same number of workers coming out as went in dis morning, den dey happy. Dough dey're never really happy."

"Hmm." Holly hummed to herself. "They count everybody. Well that's one good thing about them."

Landon rolled his eyes. "Oh, stop."

They climbed down to the next tier, helping each other safely make the drop. As they tramped along the ledge, not too quickly so as to draw attention but fast enough to gain on the dwindling line of workers ahead, Landon wondered how Ravusmane was doing outside the wall. And then he thought of Max, and his blood boiled. He was glad Hardy had said to keep Vates's staff; the gnarled wood felt good in his grasp.

Hardy stepped alongside him. "We heard a rumor on de rocks today." He kept his eyes on the curving path ahead, and Landon did the same.

"Oh? What rumor?"

"Dat anoder has come. Anoder like you from de outer realm."

Landon's boiling blood now chilled to ice.

"Max," he said through gritted teeth, which did indeed feel gritty.

Hardy appeared to nod in acknowledgment, although it may have just been an exaggerated head bounce as they walked.

"Max," he echoed. "We have one named Max, too." He gave Landon a sidelong glance. "Remember?"

Landon thought back. "Oh. . .yeah. Longshot. Maple-Tree Max! The Hundred-to-One Odd." He was the first valley person Landon had encountered on his first visit to Wonderwood. Back then, the valley people were called Odds. Max had shot arrows at Landon and Melech from a maple tree. "How's Max doing? Where is he now?"

"He work de next shift. Might see him at de top. No shooting arrows anymore." Hardy said this sadly, as if no one was doing what they used to do—or liked to do—anymore.

Near the back of the line walked Melech, his dark brown coat sprinkled gray from dust. Landon stepped more quickly, resisting the growing itch to run to his most trusted friend. Hardy, seeming to sense Landon's urge, lightly touched his arm. But then Hardy called out in a voice that made Landon flinch—

"Horsy! Yeah, you! Get to de back of de line where you belong."

Landon looked at Hardy in bewilderment, taking his eyes off the trail. When Hardy's tough face turned his way, Landon was about to scold him. But then Hardy's expression softened, and he winked. Landon couldn't help smiling.

Melech allowed the few workers behind him to pass, and then he continued walking at the back of the line. As soon as Landon reached him, the horse softly neighed. "Good to see you, young Landon."

Landon's smile broadened. Risking being noticed, he patted Melech's flank. "It's great to see you, Melech. Although I wish our circumstances were different." Landon removed his hand and stared ahead.

"Indeed. Perhaps now that you're here, our circumstances will soon be different." It sounded like both a question and a statement.

"We're here, too," Bridget said excitedly. She playfully swatted at Melech's tail until Landon gave her a stern look.

"Ah, little Miss Bridget and Holly." Melech neighed and snorted delightfully. "So good. So good. Our circumstances seem to be improving already."

Though Melech sounded sincere, Landon could sense a note of sadness beneath his tone. Yet even in a dusty rock quarry ruled by a dragon and wicked Arcans, it was good to be with old friends again.

Trudging up the rim, they talked more about the situation here. There was not enough time to get the whole history of what had happened in the valley. Basically, a short time after the animals had returned from the Island of Arcanum, the Arcans had followed, also arriving by sea. Fighting broke out soon enough, and losses were sustained on both sides. The battling continued, and as the valley people regained their fighting skills of old, the tide began to turn their way. Until Volucer Ignis showed up.

"Dere's no defense to stop him, and no attack dat can harm him," said Hardy.

"At least none that we have discovered," said Melech. Again, Landon heard more than what the horse was actually saying. Landon detected a trace of hope, hope that seemed directed toward him and his sisters.

"He must have some weakness," said Landon. "There must be some way to stop him."

Gravel crunched beneath their feet. They trudged heavily both in foot and in thought. Hardy also disclosed what seemed obvious, that Volucer Ignis had forced the valley people into slavery to mine the earth—who knew there was a rock quarry beneath the Echoing Green?—for stone, which they used to build the wall and its towers.

The hazy glow of the sky drew close overhead. They were nearing the top of the vast pit. Shadowy figures loomed at the edge, watching as the workers march woefully by.

"Four hundret twenty-two. Four hundret twenty-tree. Four hundret twenty-*horsy*."

An Arcan gave Melech a swift kick, sending him stumbling sideways, snorting. The Arcans were even taller than Landon remembered. And—he couldn't help looking—they had real eyes this time. Well, they still looked eerily nonhuman. These were big, black, glossy orbs as before, but there were thin red circles outlining large glaring pupils. It felt like someone had poured ice cubes down Landon's back when he looked at them, and he quickly averted his eyes.

"Four hundred twenty-*four*," resumed the counting Arcan, skipping Melech's number. "Four hundred twenty. . .*wait*."

Hardy had just passed by. Only Landon, Holly, and Bridget remained. No one else was behind them. The Arcan who had kicked Melech stepped before Landon, patting a sword against his long, alien hand.

"What have we here?"

Landon gripped the staff, wishing it were his sword. Without lifting his eyes, Landon noticed the Arcan was wearing armor. It was beautiful armor, and he knew in an instant that it had been fashioned by the valley people. Anger burned inside Landon. So did fear.

There was a commotion behind the Arcan. A scuffling and growling followed by a clinking *snap*.

Ravusmane. Landon's heart felt ripped in half. *No.* At least he wasn't dead. But what were they doing to him?

"Yup, that's them. The traitors."

The Arcan stepped aside, looming within reach. Landon looked up to see Maximillian Westmoreland holding Ravusmane on a chain. Max yanked the leash, jolting Ravusmane's head and causing him to wobble. The wolf had a limp. He'd been wounded.

"But where did your pretty armor go, hmm?"

Landon narrowed his eyes. His face was twitching and contorting uncontrollably.

Max smiled. "It must be down there somewhere. Who wants to go take a look?" He glanced up at either Arcan nearby. The one not bearing a sword—the counter—gave a curt nod. "I'm sure Volucer Ignis would like to see their armor."

Bridget was whimpering. Landon tried to shield her from the sight of Ravusmane, but then Max handed the chain to the Arcan.

"Take him with you. He could use the exercise." He kicked Ravusmane's bad leg, and the wolf crumpled with a yelp. "Get up, doggy! That's what you get for peeing on the wall."

The Arcan stepped around Landon, half pulling, half dragging Ravusmane behind him. Landon met Ravusmane's eyes and swallowed back tears. Bridget cried sharply, and Holly embraced her.

"Why?" said Landon, digging his fingernails into the staff. Despite his trembling rage, another question rose above the others. A question of pure puzzlement and curiosity. "How?" His face continued to twist beyond his control. "How did you—"

Max was laughing. He was laughing so hard he was shaking. He pointed at Landon, agitating him all the more.

"You should see yourself. All three of you. Man, you look funny." His laughter stopped. "Bind them," he said, and scowling at Bridget's whimpering, he added, "and gag them. All except *him*."

Max crooked a finger at Landon and stepped toward him. Landon wrinkled his nose at the boy's stench.

"You think you're the only one who's been here before? Everyone's seen you, of course, Mr. Hero Boy." Max sneered at Hardy and Melech as an Arcan jammed a bit into Melech's mouth. "I've been stealthy, you see. Lurking *in the shadows*."

Landon's heart wanted to jump out of his rib cage. He felt helpless, watching his sisters and friends being gagged.

"You're an idiot," he told Max.

Max snickered. "Yeah. Sure looks like I'm the stupid one now, huh. How about we go meet the bossman of this joint? I'm *sure* Volucer Ignis will be delighted to see you."

"Wait," said Landon. Where his boldness came from he wasn't sure, other than that he wasn't about to let this kid get the best of him. "How did you get caught in that rope—remember, back on the tree? I mean, how did that happen?"

A flash of concern or confusion gripped Max's face, but then it passed. "Oh, that. That stupid library always gives me problems. It's given my whole family problems."

Landon tried to hide his smirk.

Max sneered at him, breathing into his face. "Thanks for cutting me down, by the way. Without your help, I might have been a goner out there." He was about to turn when he added maliciously, "Your head makes a great stepladder, by the way."

Other Arcans had gathered. At Max's command, they formed a horseshoe around Landon, Holly, and Bridget and began to usher them forward. "You escaped my fire," said Max, tilting his head, "but you won't escape my master's." He glowered at them and turned to stride across the scrubby courtyard. The Arcans closed around their prisoners like a noose.

Chapter Sixteen

Rather than seeing a newly constructed city inside the wall, Landon saw what looked like a site of ancient ruins. Structures made of piled stones stood everywhere, but many of them were only half finished or were already falling apart. Some were marked by black, streaky scorch marks. Landon was afraid to discover what had happened to those places. The whole area was depressing, made even more forlorn by the towering wall closing them in and cutting off what was left of a once breathtaking forest.

People stood watching Landon and the other captives go by in silence. It felt like a funeral procession, Landon thought grimly.

"Get those slaves down to work," Max yelled at two Arcans standing idly, watching them pass by. "The rock isn't going to mine itself." Max glanced back at Landon and winked, grinning. Max apparently thought his joke was funny, or he was enjoying showing off to Landon and his gang. Probably both, Landon figured.

The two Arcans sprang into action, pushing and shoving the coverall-clad slaves. The others fell into line behind them like they'd done this a thousand times. Their heads bowed and their feet shuffling, the next shift of workers set off toward the pit.

Through open windows and doorways Landon saw other people working in the buildings. They appeared to be making more uniforms and other items Landon couldn't see or guess at. Armored Arcans loomed everywhere. Landon shuddered at the sight of the animal skulls atop their ghastly helmets, thinking of animals being released into the forest only to be shot by arrow, stabbed by sword, or burned by fire.

Between the work buildings appeared housing units, which were even scrubbier than the work buildings. Beyond these small "villages" came smells and noises from animals—hundreds or thousands—presumably penned or caged. They were worse off here than on the Island of Arcanum, thought Landon sadly. At least there they'd been under a spell and unaware of their imprisonment. Here, if they understood anything, it was that they were being held captive against their will and their instincts.

Landon's face was twitching from revulsion and anger. This place was disgusting. He'd distrusted Maximillian Westmoreland from the start, but he still couldn't believe Max would throw his lot in with the likes of Volucer Ignis and these awful Arcans.

The line of workers continued to shuffle in the opposite direction. Landon's heart sank more with each tired, lost face he saw. Most didn't look his way. Those who did, however briefly, risked being jabbed by a stick or whacked with the broadside of a sword. Each time an Arcan acted violently, Landon winced.

Bridget was softly whimpering. Landon's anger subsided as compassion filled his heart. He stepped alongside his youngest sister. Holly already had an arm around her from the other side. Scraping his shoes across the gravel to cover his voice, Landon whispered, "It's. . .okay." He squeezed Bridget's shoulder.

Strange words, Landon realized, when nothing was okay at all. Still, what else could one say?

Max abruptly stopped and spun around, a frown gripping his face. "Hey! No talking." He strode toward them until he was face-to-face with Landon. "And let go of her." His eyes darted to Bridget and back.

Landon's heartbeat quickened. His throat felt thick with emotion. "Make me."

Hardy and Melech stepped closer, but the surrounding Arcans immediately cut them off with wielded swords. Melech was snorting and Hardy grumbling through his gag.

"Shut it!" Max said, glaring at them. The Arcans pushed Hardy and Melech farther back, clicking their crossed swords as a barrier.

When Max looked back at him, Landon could see the uncertainty in the boy's eyes. Max's mouth twitched, and then the skin around his left eye tightened. A tic. Landon wondered if he had him scared, even as he felt his own heart bouncing inside his ribs like an animal trying to escape from its cage.

After at least a minute during which neither Landon nor Max blinked, Max's eyes finally flipped like shutters.

"All right," he said. His nostrils flared like a bull's about to charge. "Have it your way."

Before he'd finished speaking, Max had raised his arms, formed a club with his fists, and was bringing it down toward Bridget's shoulder to break Landon's grip.

Landon lunged to his left, shoving his sisters away while raising Vates's staff to thwart the blow.

Max's club hammered down, crashing the staff against Landon's chest and sending both boys reeling to the ground. Before Max could deliver another blow, this time aiming a punch at Landon's face, Landon cast the staff aside and caught Max's arm. Something on the underside of Max's forearm drew Landon's attention. A crude, ugly mark of a skull and crossbones ringed by fire had been burned into Max's flesh.

Landon gasped both at the tattoo and because he realized Max's other—free—hand was soaring into view from the left. Just before impact, an ear-piercing shriek split the air. Max froze and then looked up. His fist remained hovering an inch from Landon's jaw. After another screech from the sky, Max looked at Landon. Slowly drawing his fist away, he yanked his other arm from Landon's grasp and then stood looming over him. A peculiar expression came over Max's face. It was a look that Landon couldn't precisely read.

"He doesn't want damaged goods," said Max, scoffing.

"Who?" said Landon. "The dragon?" Clouds swirled overhead, spiraling after an unseen flyer.

Max glanced at Vates's staff on the ground. He snatched it up and began walking. "Come on," he said. His voice sounded flat. It seemed he was now simply obeying orders. "Volucer Ignis wants to see us. All of us." Max clicked Vates's staff along the stones.

Landon wanted to protest Max using Vates's walking stick, but after looking at Hardy and Melech, who were remaining terribly quiet, Landon decided to take his cue from them and just go along for now.

The wall along their left-hand side rose to a dizzying height. Several giant towers popped into view, each topped by a turret. *The Whump Trees,* thought Landon sadly, *covered in stone.* He felt fairly certain he would never see those wondrous trees again.

The party veered away from the wall across more stony ground. *There should be trees here, as well,* Landon thought. Landon had the feeling they were heading toward the place where he and Melech had first entered Wonderwood long, long ago. The fall from the giant chessboard in the sky, the walk along the cliff, the funny poem called "The Weigh Down"—the memory of it made Landon's knees tremble.

He noticed another rock quarry, even larger than the one near the wall, although it was totally empty. The huge, gaping hole in the earth was like a lonely grave.

Ahead of them, the broken courtyard changed drastically. They neared a magnificent archway guarded by large Arcans wearing golden armor. The guards stood still as statues on either side of the entryway as Max led the prisoners through. Beyond the archway the sight grew more amazing. If the outer yards were shabby and rundown, this courtyard was stately and fit for a king.

Or a dragon.

Gold and silver filigree ornamented everything from stone-work to pillars to metal sculptures that were both frightening and exhilarating to behold. Vates's staff clicked and tapped regularly along the polished checkerboard marble patio. Max seemed to be thoroughly enjoying his possession of the stick. As they crossed the courtyard toward a strange, castlelike structure, a flash of light and heat from the right caused Landon to jump. From what appeared to be a giant dragon's mouth, flames spewed out. Beyond the flames, Landon saw a long tongue projecting over the ground, and on the tongue were shiny metallic objects rolling away from the creature's gaping jaws.

The dragon's head was actually chiseled metalwork. The protruding tongue was a conveyor belt-type contraption, and the shiny objects seemed to be swords, shields, and pieces of armor, which crashed and clanged to the marble floor upon reaching the end of the belt. When the last piece had fallen, the dragon's mouth closed, concealing the fire except through its eyes, where the flames flickered angrily.

Max led them up long steps that resembled the climb to an ancient Aztec temple. At the top, the space before them stretched high, deep, and cavernous. Outside light barely crept past the first soaring pillars, which were so enormous the entire party of captors and prisoners couldn't have completed a ring around one of them. Had they moved some of the Whump Trees here to serve as foundations for these columns, as well? But how could they possibly have moved any of those trees?

Unseen birds—or bats—flew high overhead. Were other

animals lurking in the shadows? As they marched inside the fortress, Landon could only see a few feet around him in any direction. That was all. The rest of the place was lost to darkness. Landon realized he was holding someone's hand. He gently squeezed, seeing Bridget faintly beside him. On her other side walked Holly. Landon met her eyes and forced a smile. Oddly he realized he wasn't feeling afraid. He felt mostly numb, as if this were a passing dream from which he might awaken any moment.

Any moment now, he thought, giving Bridget's hand another squeeze.

She squeezed back.

Any moment. . .

A line of fire shot across the darkness, leaving a blazing ball floating in midair. Another streak shot in the other direction, lighting another ball. They weren't floating fireballs, however, but tall, giant torches.

"Not for my benefit," murmured a voice. "But for yours."

Landon squinted, at first seeing only the blazing torches. Soon the light caught the one who had spoken. *Volucer Ignis.*

The dragon was half sitting, half lounging across a wide, gigantic throne. His grayish-brown skin (it was hard to distinguish color in this light) heaved with his breathing. Landon could feel the hot air radiating from his nostrils, even at a distance.

"Impressive, isn't it?"

At first Landon thought the dragon wasn't even looking at them. Then with a shiver—despite the heavy warmth of the place—he realized the dragon was indeed looking at them. He was studying them askance with one eye, the only eye facing them. The narrowed eye reflected yellow and red light from the torches, although Landon thought he detected a green glint when the eye passed his way. It was chilling.

"So, Maximillian, you finally brought your friends to play."

Max dipped one knee, almost like a curtsy. "Yes, Master."

Master? Landon suddenly felt claustrophobic, despite the arena-like space around them.

"Then I suppose we should bring out the others, as well."

"Yes, Master."

Max moved so quickly he almost stumbled over Vates's staff, as if he'd forgotten he was holding it. He ran off at an angle into the shadows behind the right-hand torch. Landon had the impression he was watching a show or a play, and the dragon was the featured act on stage. Max had just run into the wing to get some other entertainers onstage. The people he returned with, however, were no actors. The sight of them made Landon's heart both leap and sink at the same time. Here came Vates, Ditty, Griggs and Dot—Ditty's parents—Battleroot, Wagglewhip, and finally, Ludo. All but Ludo were chained together and gagged. Ludo nevertheless walked just as heavily.

"Come on up here, Ludificor. Come on, come on." The more the dragon spoke, the more his voice was getting inside Landon's head. A giant claw, which Landon hadn't before noticed, tapped the floor. *Tick! Tick! Tick!*

Ludo was dressed much as he had been when Landon had first met him, except everything appeared rumpled and torn—his top hat (which had been crumpled during Landon's first visit, if this was the same one), waistcoat trailing long tails, a fancy white (or at least light-colored) shirt, knee-length pants, and whitish socks. Seeing Ludo climb the steps toward Volucer Ignis struck such a deep note of sadness in Landon's heart he almost couldn't bear to watch.

The dragon's single visible eye settled on Landon. The black pupil narrowed to a slit, pinching the breath from Landon's lungs.

"Yes," the dragon hissed. "Ludificor Stultus. Once a fool, always a fool. Once weak, always weak." Ludo had reached the summit and stopped awkwardly on the top step. He seemed about to teeter and tumble right back down. Landon could scarcely breathe. Bridget's hand clamped his like a vise.

"He's told me all about you." Landon knew the dragon was speaking to him. "Oh, I can't really be everywhere, yet my presence is everywhere felt. And I can't really know everything, yet I always find out what I need."

Landon thought he was about to pass out. He was grateful for Bridget's clutching hand. It gave him something to focus on. Something real and right and true. Landon spread his fingers to loosen her grip momentarily, and then he slid his fingers between hers.

Max came panting back into view. "The others," he said, leaning on Vates's staff.

Landon tried to catch Vates's eye. The old man looked more ancient than ever. Still, the sight of him touched Landon's soul with hope. Ditty was looking Landon's way, and when their eyes met, Landon actually felt his lips curve upward. *Yes, there is hope.* His friends reminded him of the Auctor's presence. And where the Auctor was, hope always reigned. But was the Auctor really here with them in this dark, gloomy place?

The dragon turned his monstrous head. With his gaze full on, Landon took a half step back. Fear began scratching at his heart. Volucer Ignis seemed to notice Landon's and Ditty's response to each other.

"Weak fools are always useful." Volucer Ignis crossed his eyes at Ludo, who trembled pitifully under the dragon's gaze. Suddenly, Ludo faced Landon and the others, screaming, "Please forgive! I don't want to live!"

Two wings rose like ragged black sails, and the dragon's claw lashed like a monstrous cat's paw, reaching both longer and quicker than seemed possible, batting Ludo from the step clear to the black recess near the wall. A faint cry echoed. Then it was silent.

"Useful for a while," continued Volucer Ignis, retracting his leg as if he'd just stretched after a nap. "But too easy."

Max had dropped to both knees at the base of the steps, either out of admiration and respect or to offer a smaller target for his master. Surely the dragon couldn't reach him all the way down there. Of course, the dreadful creature could reach anywhere with only a flap or two of his horrid wings.

Landon heard a soft whimper, though it didn't come from across the hall. Bridget had stayed remarkably quiet until this moment. Even though she said nothing, Landon heard in her cry a plea for help. For someone to do something.

Landon swallowed, giving her hand a meaningful squeeze before releasing it. He took a step forward.

"I'm not afraid."

The words came out, and they sounded pretty good from what Landon could tell. But the scratch of fear along his heart now became a claw ripping at his chest.

"You can't hurt us."

Now wait a second. Where did *that* come from? Had he really just said that to this huge dragon who had just flicked Ludo into the air like a crumb from a tabletop?

Volucer Ignis perked up. His breathing increased, warming the room.

"Oh, good. I was so hoping you would play. Now what makes you think I can't hurt you?"

Landon blinked. His eyes were beginning to sting. There was smoke in the room, he realized, though he couldn't see it too well.

"Because you're just a made-up creature," said Landon.

The dragon snorted, and Landon saw another gauzelike layer of smoke settling in the room.

"Made-up, as in *created*?"

"Yes," said Landon. "We saw the fire on the Island of Arcanum. They made you there with some strange alchemy—"

The wings were up and beating. Landon could hardly hear himself over the rush of wind. The torches blew sideways, threatening to go out.

"Not another fool!" The dragon lolled his head before leveling his gaze at Landon. "I have enough fools, Landon Snow. No. Now I have my eyes on a prize." His eyes slid over Landon's sisters and his friends. "Prizes and trinkets. But don't disappoint me again. Think. Aren't you smarter than *that?*"

The beast sounded truly upset. Landon felt his face tighten into a frown. It felt like someone had gripped his head on either side and was pressing inward. An idea popped out. His face relaxed. But his relief at realizing the truth was short-lived.

"They didn't make you," he spoke as if to himself. "*You* made *them.*"

The dragon sighed. "Very good. But that was close. I'm afraid you're going to have to impress me with something more than that. That should have been a given."

Landon had the uncanny feeling he was sitting down across from someone about to play a game of chess. This inkling grew into a competitive urge. It was time to turn the table and ask their captor a question.

"Why did you want me—want *us*—to come here?"

Volucer Ignis settled back into his half lounging position across the throne. It really didn't look very comfortable, but the dragon revealed no sign of discomfort. Did such a dragon even experience comfort or discomfort?

"To play," said Volucer Ignis. "And to join me as your friend Max has."

"He's not my friend." Landon couldn't keep the acid tone from his voice.

"Not yet, perhaps. I suspect you'll be friends soon enough, however. Soon enough."

The dragon's voice trailed off, and he released a very visible puff of smoke through his nostrils.

Landon glared at the back of Max's stooped form. "I don't

think so," said Landon, bile churning in his stomach. "No. Never."

Volucer Ignis blew another stream of smoke. It was beginning to get quite thick and hazy. The beast's green eyes glinted through the cloud. "Right," he drawled. "Now I've told you why I wanted you to come, so why don't you tell me why *you* wanted to come see me."

"To set the people free," said Landon boldly.

"Mnph-mnph!" said Bridget.

"Oh, and the animals, too, of course," Landon added.

The dragon choked, though it sounded like a laugh. "Free? What is free?" His wings lifted and fell as gently as a butterfly's on a flower. "Oh, that's rich. That's rich indeed. It looks like I may get my wish after all. You *have* come to play." He choked again, rasping so deep and hard that Landon couldn't help cringing. "And how do you propose to accomplish this for which you have come? This, this *freedom*." This time, his choking laughter made Landon mad.

"By destroying you," said Landon.

The choking stopped. Volucer Ignis folded his wings flat and looked at Landon. Even Max was craning his neck to peek back at him. Landon could feel his heart pounding at the top of his chest.

The dragon spoke. "You don't know who you're trifling with, boy." The green eyes narrowed, and the hideous head slowly bobbed. "But you're more like me than I'd guessed. And that's good. Yessss—very good. Do you know what you've got?" His voice rose to send the word *got* echoing down the hall.

Landon flinched. He tried raising his voice, but it came out in a squeak. "What?"

If a dragon could smile, that's what Volucer Ignis did before shouting, "Fire!"

Landon hit the deck with everyone else as a blanket of fire burned overhead. The heat dissipated as quickly as it had arrived. Landon cautiously lifted his head. The dragon was still grinning, jutting several pointed teeth. The beast opened his jaws. "Still want to play?"

Melech was stamping and whinnying while Hardy patted at Melech's neck, where his mane had been singed. The burnt hair stench reached Landon's nose. Clenching his fists, he focused to keep his emotions in check.

"Still want to play?" Volucer Ignis repeated sweetly.

Landon nodded, blinking hard against the smoke.

"Good. I'll give you ten tries."

Landon coughed and cleared his throat. "To destroy you?"

The dragon laughed, a deep rumbling that shook the floor. "That would be entertaining, I suppose. But I'll make it easier for you."

Landon rubbed his eyes, waiting.

"I'll give you ten tries to *impress* me. That's all."

Landon again waited, not sure how to respond. He got to his knees and stood. "And if I succeed, then all the people—and the animals—get to go free?" he asked finally.

The dragon snorted. "Oh, but of course! If you succeed." He punctuated *if* with a huffy sniff.

Landon knew the dragon was lying. His friends in chains still lay on the ground near the bottom step. Holly and Bridget sat on the floor behind him. Hardy was patting Melech gently now, only to calm him. They looked at Landon; everyone seemed to be turning to him except for Max, who lay prostrate before the dragon's throne. Slowly they all began to nod. Hardy and Melech, Bridget and Holly, Vates and Griggs and Dot, Battleroot and Wagglewhip, and Ditty. Vates raised his cuffed wrists and then bowed his head. Ditty did the same. A few others imitated them.

They're praying, Landon thought. A wave of strength flowed through him.

"But *when* you *fail*," Volucer Ignis sniffed, "you and your sisters will stay with me. . .forever."

Landon looked at Holly and Bridget, and they looked at him. Then they closed their eyes and lowered their heads. Landon turned to face his challenger.

"I accept."

onfidence is a fickle and funny thing, Landon discovered in that moment standing before Volucer Ignis. With the support of his friends, and sensing the strength and presence of the Auctor—who was the only One who could get them all out of this situation—it had been easy to utter those two words in response to the dragon's challenge: "I accept."

As soon as the words left his lips, however, Landon felt a great whooshing sensation, like a deflating balloon. He suddenly felt empty and spent. What's more, his brain drained of any thoughts or ideas. What in the world could he do to impress a giant, wicked beast like Volucer Ignis? What was he thinking? After standing there stupidly for what seemed an eternity, Landon heard the dragon tapping his claw.

Tick.

Tick.

Tick.

It was like a timer counting down toward Landon's doom.

"Well?" said the dragon. "This isn't very impressive so far." He swung his massive head and yawned, lighting the air with a breath of fire.

Landon pointed at Max. "Get up, Max."

The boy appeared to be either dead or sleeping. He certainly wasn't praying like the others were. Had he fainted?

Volucer Ignis cast one eye his way.

Max slowly stood.

"Hold out the staff," said Landon.

At the dragon's half nod, Max obeyed and thrust out his arm, raising Vates's staff. No sooner had his arm straightened than the long stick went limp and began to curl and curve in the air.

"Augh!" Max dropped the snake and jumped away. The serpent began climbing the steps—a long, oily line defying gravity. As the snake slithered onto the platform, Volucer Ignis turned his head, flicked his lizardlike tongue, and gulped the snake down.

"An appetizer," said the dragon before burping through jagged teeth. A puff of smoke went up. "But not very impressive."

Landon heard a gurgle behind him. It was Holly. "Mm-mmh!"

He thought she probably meant "Moses." He took this as encouragement that he was on the right track.

How had Moses and Aaron convinced Pharaoh to let the Israelites go? *The ten plagues on Egypt.* Landon felt worried. Changing Aaron's staff into a serpent hadn't been one of the plagues. It had been a warm-up exercise. *An appetizer.* Landon gulped. Had it even been Aaron's staff? Or was it Moses'? Landon frowned. His mind was drawing blanks again. Meanwhile Volucer Ignis had resumed tapping his claw.

Tick.

Tick.

Stop that! Landon wanted to shout. He closed his eyes, trying to breathe. What else had Moses done? What were the other plagues? *All I need to do is impress him,* thought Landon. One of the plagues ought to impress an evil dragon, right?

Landon opened his eyes to see Max standing off to the side. At least *he* had been impressed. Normally, seeing Max jump like that would have brought some joy to Landon's heart. Right now, however, he felt mounting pressure and concern.

"Hm *hm*-hmm." Holly tried to speak through her gag. "Hngh hngh-*hngh*."

The river? thought Landon. Turned to blood?

Yes, that had been the first plague. But how could he apply that here?

"Do you have some water?" he asked Volucer Ignis.

The dragon hesitated, seeming to question Landon's intent. "Of course," he said finally. At a flick of his claw, two Arcans scampered from the hall. They returned shortly, bearing a large golden bowl. Landon blinked at the shimmering metal, shiny on the outside and glistening beneath the water. It was a very impressive bowl. But he wasn't the one to be impressed here. He pretended it was a plain aluminum mixing bowl like his mother used.

Then he realized the staff was gone. Vates's staff had been eaten! Landon sighed. This was not going so well, not well at all.

Out of desperation he closed his eyes, asked for help, waved his hands over the bowl, and then opened his eyes again. The water had turned into blood! Landon stumbled backward, covering his mouth at the revolting sight.

"Behold the bowl!" he said, gesturing as he continued backing away from it. "Behold the *blood*!"

Volucer Ignis stepped from his throne and peered down. He looked like a giant leathery gargoyle perched outside a museum. He lashed out his tongue, dipping it mothlike into the bowl, splattering blood and slurping it into his mouth. Landon's throat tightened as he forced himself not to throw up. He hoped Bridget, at least, wasn't watching this.

"Food *and* drink. A bit tasty, but not impressive." With a lurching heave, the dragon beat his wings—*whoosh*—and dropped back onto his throne. "That's two." His massive shoulders slumped with a sigh. One leg—or was it an arm?—hung casually toward the floor. The dragon dragged his claw back and forth along the stone floor—*scritch, scritch*—grating on Landon's nerves like fingernails on a chalkboard.

Two down, thought Landon, and the dragon wasn't at all impressed? What would it take?

Scritch, scritch.

Landon gritted his teeth and clenched his fists. He wanted to scream for Volucer Ignis to stop. He didn't think he could take it anymore. And since he could think of no other feats to try, he yelled the next plague that came to mind.

"Darkness!"

The torches extinguished. The darkness was so inky and

black, Landon thought he could feel it weighing down on him, pressing against his body and his eyes like a heavy blanket. Or, Landon thought, *like pitch*. This was the first time he truly understood that term, pitch black. Like liquid tar, blackness poured in everywhere, filling the space with invisibility.

Something moved in it, breathing. "Now I like this, as it is my natural element. Like putting a fish in water. Am I impressed? No. But I do feel right at home."

Landon couldn't tell where the dragon was. His voice seemed to float around him, rippling in every direction like a circle growing from a stone dropped into smooth water. Landon didn't think *he* had moved. But it was easy to lose one's bearing in such darkness. There was no reference point for anything. Finally, Landon clapped his hands twice—*smack, smack*—and he prayed aloud, "Light! Please, let there be light!"

The torches sizzled to life like twin beacons across a black sea. "Thank you," Landon sighed. His chest was heaving, hyperventilating.

"What was that?" Volucer Ignis was still lounging across the throne, apparently having not moved an inch.

"Nothing," said Landon.

"No, that was something. That was light, which makes for try number four." The dragon sighed, and Landon could hear the "ho-hum" in his tone. "Really, Landon, I was hoping for something original, at least. Snakes, blood, darkness, light— haven't these all been played with before?"

Landon peeked at his sisters. Thank goodness, they both had their eyes closed. Hopefully they'd been that way through the darkness, which wouldn't have made it so bad. Even Hardy's eyes were closed, and Melech's. Had they all given up on him? Did they realize, as Landon was suspecting, that their fate was sealed no matter what sort of show he put on for Volucer Ignis? *"There's no winning with a dragon,"* Landon imagined Hardy or perhaps Vates saying. *"There's only playing until he becomes too bored. And then there's losing."*

The dragon flexed his limbs like a giant cat with reptilian scales, opening wide his jaws in a yawn. He had become too bored to tap or scratch the floor. Was he going to sleep?

A jerk of chains caught Landon's attention. Vates was struggling as if trying to say something. Volucer Ignis cast a weary eye toward the group in chains. "Ungag the haggard wretch," he said, his eye sliding toward his claw. An Arcan obeyed, removing the cloth from the old man's mouth.

At first Vates only coughed and spat, and Landon was afraid he might pass out or even die. How miserable this had to be for everyone! Finally, the old prophet looked at Landon, his eyes dim shadows beneath the wavering torchlight. His voice came surprisingly strong and clear, however, the mere sound of it cheering Landon and emboldening him.

"Let us stop this foolishness," said Vates, drawing at least a curious glance from the dragon. "Not at ten," Vates continued, "but at five."

Volucer Ignis turned and sat upright on the throne. Strangely, this made Landon feel better, at least for the moment.

"A parley, eh?" said the dragon. "That doesn't count as impressive in itself, and it didn't come from the boy"—he eyeballed

Landon—"but I'll say this much for the haggard man's tactic. It's intriguing. So, what are the stakes?"

Volucer Ignis and Vates both stared at Landon. Stakes? Landon wondered. What stakes? What else was there besides the people's—and the animals'—freedom?

"Well," said the dragon, still eyeing him, "you've upped the ante, so I assume you'd also like to raise the stakes." He said this as if it had been Landon, and not Vates, who had come up with the idea.

"Uh," Landon stalled. He was looking to Vates for help, but the old man seemed to have gone mute. Did Vates simply want to get the whole thing over with more quickly to put them out of their misery? That would be merciful. However, Landon had a feeling that's not what Vates was doing. It was something else. Landon thought hard. In a flash of inspiration, he saw it. "The wall."

"The wall?" Volucer Ignis inclined his head. His wings popped out and were flitting ever so subtly, as if he were warming up for something. "What about it?"

"It comes down," said Landon definitively. "I impress you with my next try, the people and animals are set free, and the wall comes down. All of it."

One of Volucer Ignis's eyes appeared to open wider than the other. If he'd had eyebrows, he'd have been raising one at Landon. "Intriguing and interesting." He studied Landon, pondering something. Landon coughed.

"Well?" said the dragon. "Go ahead."

Landon's heart pounded. He needed more time. It seemed

right to maintain the dragon's interest, to keep him piqued, but Landon had no idea what he was supposed to do.

"It's not me who will impress you," said Landon, wondering if that was grammatically correct. *Not I?* It didn't matter. "I can't do it. But the Auctor will."

Silence thick as darkness filled the room. Volucer Ignis remained still except for his hovering wings. The ragged black membranes were trembling. At first Landon thought it was from fear. But he was mistaken. It was due to rage.

"Do not mention that. . .name. . .again. Ever. Do you understand?"

Landon shivered, and it was all he could do to keep from nodding.

"Say it again, and the game is over. You will all be—how do you say?—toast." The dragon's nostrils became dual flamethrowers for effect. Landon winced from the heat. "I'll turn your animal friends into crispy critters."

Bridget screamed through her gag.

Landon knew this was it. He had one more chance *(Thanks a lot, Vates)*, one more try, one final shot to impress Volucer Ignis. But it was only a game. He was playing against an evil dragon. There was no possible victory here.

Then again. . .

Landon looked around. He thought of the hundreds of people working in the quarry, laboring in slavery for this wicked beast. Looking at Bridget, pitifully bound and gagged, he thought of the thousands of helpless animals existing in fear, released from captivity only to be hunted down for sport. They weren't even used for food or clothing, so far as he could tell. Only their skulls were used to adorn the Arcans' headgear.

They're praying for me, Landon thought. *My friends are asking the Auctor for help. I'm not alone.*

Vates was right. The time for playing was over. It was time to pick a fight. Still without a clue as to what he would actually do, other than keep praying really, really hard, Landon spoke words he'd heard only in movies and on TV. "Let's take this outside."

Volucer Ignis hesitated, but only for a moment. "Let's do, me and you."

Vates was shaking his head.

"No," said Landon. "All of us. Everyone here, and all the workers, both in the quarry and out. And—" Landon smirked "—all of the animals. Every person and creature you're holding captive in these walls, I want with me outside."

The dragon's head drooped so far to one side Landon thought he would tumble from his throne. With a blazing snort, his head snapped back up. "The more the merrier. Let them all see you fail."

Vates stared at Landon. Did he want to tell him something? Was there a plan or idea he'd had in mind? Or had he lost his mind? Were they all going out to their doom? Well, they may not be going out in a blaze of glory, but they would surely go out in a blaze.

"Rub some soot!" Vates shouted, his voice echoing down the chamber. "Remember the sign, Landon. The cliff! The Way Down may be—"

"What?" Volucer Ignis bellowed angrily. "Shut him up!"

The dragon's long tail flew like a scorpion's, striking a torch into a burst of fireworks. "Rub some soot on *him*!"

Landon gasped, stifling a scream as the Arcans gagged Vates, shoved him to the floor, and showered him with handfuls of still-glowing ash. Vates's cries pained Landon's heart. Sparks fell on everyone, burning Dot and Griggs and Ditty, Wagglewhip and Battleroot, but mostly poor Vates.

Tears welled in the pits of Landon's eyes. As his emotions ran through him, he pondered Vates's words, remembering the strange sign with the words of soot on them. It seemed so long ago. Finally, his anger at the dragon got the best of him.

"Outside," Landon said in a voice deeper than his years. "Now."

Volucer Ignis flared his eyes and scratched the floor, tearing it apart. The dragon leaped, tossing chunks of stone. Hovering, he beat his wings and lunged, filling the air with sparks and dust.

People moaned and choked on their gags in the dragon's wake. The Arcans had them on their feet, prodding them down the dim corridor. As they passed by, Landon wanted to reach out and touch each of them, offer them some comfort or hope. But the Arcans stepped purposefully between him and his friends, keeping them apart.

Max said in a mocking voice, " 'Rub some soot.' Ha. I rubbed lots of soot back in the fireplace in Bart the Fart's cabin. Yeah, that impressed Volucer Ignis. Rub some soot!" Max continued laughing, striding down the hall.

"You sure were quiet in here," said Landon, challenging him. "What were you, scared?"

Max wheeled around, giving him a funny look. "Stinkin' right I'm scared of him. Terrified." He smirked. "But not half as much as you're going to be outside." Turning back around, he walked haughtily off.

The Arcans surrounded Holly, Bridget, Hardy, and Melech, ushering them toward the fortress entrance. A wooshing sound accompanied two Arcans as they marched past Landon on either side, carrying the tall torches before them. Darkness chased after them, so Landon focused on the light ahead, illuminating his path. As he began to walk—alone but not alone—he pondered Vates's words. He stepped outside into dreary gray twilight, astounded to see a crowd of people and animals forming on the plaza below.

Landon paused atop the terrace of templelike steps. "Not here," he called out nervously, hoping the crowd could hear him. "Not in here! We're going to gather out there. Follow me!"

From an unseen perch, Volucer Ignis suddenly swooped into view. "You're trying my patience, Snow," he hissed, bobbing in the air.

"It's my last try," said Landon. "And then it will all be over."

The dragon's jaws snapped like a bear trap and grinned. "You've got that much right," he said. Spewing a column of fire into the air, he climbed after it and then plunged toward the crowd. "Follow the boy!" he bellowed, causing the masses to sway like waves as he glided overhead. Soaring upward, he came back toward Landon upside down before completing a full loop. "To the bitter end!" Volucer Ignis bellowed.

Landon covered his eyes, grimacing against the throaty blast of heat.

Chapter Eighteen

Rub some soot!" Vates had said. Rub some soot.

As Landon descended the steps and marched through a parting path among the people and animals, he thought of Moses and what it must have felt like leading the Israelites out of Egypt. Had Moses also feared for his people's doom? Had he felt this much weight and responsibility upon his shoulders? *Probably he did,* thought Landon. *Although he did get to have ten goes at Pharaoh to shake him, not just five.*

Landon wasn't mad at Vates for shortening "the game," however. In fact, one way or another, he would be glad to get this whole thing over with. Besides, what would he have done with five more tries? Volucer Ignis was obviously not one who was easily impressed. And if Landon had tried some of the other plagues—locusts, frogs, gnats, flies, dust, and boils (sure, *now* he could remember them)—well, what good would that have done? At best, it probably would have only pleased or amused the dragon, and at worst, it might have bored him still more. For Landon and everyone else, well, it would have been plain gross. All those frogs? Ugh. Landon didn't even want to think about it.

He passed through the archway and veered to his left. He was going even farther from the wall in the forest. He had a feeling he was looking for something. Yes, Landon thought, *I'm looking for a sign.* But how would he ever spot it out here? If it *was* still here.

Tree stumps appeared, followed by leafless and limbless trunks, followed by scraggly trees, and finally they came to what seemed untouched forest. Large trees. Green trees. Tall trees rustling gently overhead and covering the forest floor with a canopy of intertwining branches.

Arcans issued commands in odd tongues that didn't sound like human or animal speech. The strange voices, along with the occasional *clank* of a sword or *whack* of a stick, reminded Landon that no one was freed yet, despite the refreshing change in scenery. As gradually as the forest had come back to life, it stopped abruptly. Landon stepped out to a bizarre sight indeed. A stretch of barren land lay ahead, scrubby and rocky and flat, beyond which rose prairie and in the far, far distance—hills. The wall stood as high as a cliff.

Landon's heart began to pound. To his right and to his left, the forest extended indefinitely. This was the spot, he thought excitedly. *We're close. I can feel it.*

High overhead the trees rustled and then roared, and down swooped Volucer Ignis.

"So you've come to the outer edge. Bravo, Landon Snow.

And now my patience has been exhausted. Good-bye." Before anyone else had stepped out of the forest, Volucer Ignis began igniting it from the top down. Soon dozens of gorgeous trees were blazing orange and sending up plumes of thick black smoke.

"No! Wait! I still get my last try," Landon cried.

The flow of fire ceased, though Volucer Ignis appeared far from being appeased.

Landon's eyes were searching fast. Where was it? He began pacing along the tree line, zigzagging between the trees and out on the rocky ground.

"Now what? Have you gone mad?" Volucer Ignis watched him with only mild interest. Landon half expected to be scorched at any moment. Moving quickly toward the trees and then swiveling and striding back out, Landon suddenly stopped. This wasn't what he'd been looking for. As he stood staring at it, however, he knew it had been something he'd needed to find.

Heedless of what the dragon might do or say, Landon approached not a tree, but a bush. A bush full of ripe blueberries. Without thinking, he plucked one and popped it into his mouth. The juice was succulent. Pulling another plump berry from its stem, Landon rolled it back and forth between his fingers.

"How dare you deface my forest!" The dragon roared.

From the corner of his eye, Landon saw flames coming in time to leap back from their blast. The blueberry bush combusted. Landon stared at it, saddened by this wasteful destruction. Although the bush burned, it didn't appear to *change*. The flames writhed and licked harmlessly among its branches. Even the berries remained intact.

Landon looked at Volucer Ignis. If he was impressed, he masked it beneath his heaving rage.

Holding the blueberry, Landon commanded the valley people and animals to join him outside the trees. Landon dragged his heel purposefully, searching the ground. When he found a crack, his heart leaped. He glanced in either direction. The line ran both ways. His heart pounding, Landon could hardly keep from yelling at everyone to hurry, *hurry* to his side of the crack.

Surprisingly, the dragon seemed okay with this. In fact, the more slaves and animals that gathered behind Landon, the calmer and happier he seemed. Although happy was hardly a term that could ever really apply to Volucer Ignis. When at last it appeared that everyone was there, a huge throng of people and animals standing uncertainly on the scrubby earth, Landon saw the reason for Volucer Ignis's growing satisfaction. The Arcans had lined up opposite them among the trees, each poised with a bow and arrow at the ready.

Landon had set up his friends for the firing squad.

"All right," said Volucer Ignis, pacing between the ranks like a general. He glanced at the burning blueberry bush and then eyed Landon. "That might have been impressive, but you weren't even expecting it to happen, were you? I thought not." He bowed his head and paced. "Well, I've decided to impress *myself* with your final act. You've managed to amass everyone foolish enough to follow you. Now you will all meet your fate."

Flicking his tail and twisting his head, Volucer Ignis commanded his Arcans to raise their bows.

The crowd grew tense. Facing a thousand arrows fletched and

aimed, Landon toed the edge of the crack. He looked to his left, relieved to see Ravusmane, as well as the three workers who had exchanged their coveralls with Landon and his sisters. They still wore the armor, and the thought occurred to Landon that they might be the only three to survive this point-blank assault. Hardy and Melech stood nearby. Melech stamped, drawing attention to his hooves. Beneath them four circles were scratched into the ground, in which Melech's hooves fit perfectly.

Melech bowed his head, and if not for the bit in his mouth, Landon knew what his loyal friend would say. "Young Landon, I have done my duty and am glad for it."

Landon bowed humbly back.

Holly and Bridget stared at their brother, but their eyes held no fear.

As Landon continued gazing about him, exchanging looks with Ditty and her parents and other people and creatures, some of whom he recognized and many of whom he didn't, he realized half-consciously that his fingers had been working at the blueberry in his hand. He'd been peeling away its thin skin and digging inside. Finding a hard tiny seed, he pinched it and flung the rest of the berry away.

"Wait! I'm late! I too must meet my fate!"

Everyone including Volucer Ignis turned toward the voice. Commotion broke out among the line of Arcans as a sprightly sprig of a fellow burst through. Pausing, momentarily transfixed between the two parties, Ludo finally found Landon and skipped over to him.

"Me most humblest apologies, Landon Snow. I didn't know."

Ludo's voice broke. "I didn't know!" His eyes watered as his sharp chin quivered. He bowed his head. "I am *sorry*."

"Do not *worry*," said Landon, pulling Ludo behind him. As he looked back toward the trees, he saw Max sitting on a branch over an Arcan's animal-skull-topped head. Max grinned wickedly. With compassion in his heart, Landon gestured for Max to join him. The boy only shook his head.

"And so, it is time," said Volucer Ignis, apparently still relishing the moment. With a final look at Landon, he asked him, "Any last words?"

"Yes," said Landon. Lifting his eyes from the dragon to the trees and on up to the colorless sky, he flipped the seed into the air and said, "I believe."

The blueberry seed landed on the other side of the line. Volucer Ignis watched it fall, tilting his head curiously. After a second of complete silence, the dragon shouted, "Fire!" and he flew into the air.

Between the dragon's command and the releasing of arrows, the ground beneath Landon and the people and animals of Wonderwood began to tremble and rise. The first wave of arrows bounced harmlessly off the face of the climbing cliff. After that, Landon became unaware of any arrows, as the Arcans fell far below. Landon stood teetering on the verge, spinning his arms for balance. As his knees gave way, somebody caught him and dragged him back.

Landon wanted to say thanks, but he couldn't talk. The upward thrust of the earth made him feel like a thousand pounds. Holly and Bridget sat beside him, their faces jiggling with the quake. Landon smiled, using his remaining strength to embrace them.

Over the rumbling earth came a growing roar from below. Flames shot skyward before Volucer Ignis flapped into view, hovering at cliff's edge.

"NO!" he screamed, slashing his mighty claw.

The claw struck the ground at Landon's feet, tearing away earth and rock. But then a strange thing happened. The dragon, the cliff, the sky, everything disappeared. The people and animals—the entire population of Wonderwood—suddenly vanished. But Holly and Bridget still sat beside him. They were inside some sort of wooden box or small room, and, he realized after a second, it was moving. Climbing. Rising slowly like an elevator.

The movement stopped, as did a mechanized hum. Landon and his sisters sat quietly stunned.

"What happened?" asked Bridget finally. "Where. . .where *are* we?"

The light flickered. Fastened to the back wall was an old lantern. The wall before them, Landon realized, looked like a door. He scooted toward it and pushed. It gave an inch before bumping something. "Help," said Landon.

Helping each other up—they were all feeling pretty shaky— the three of them pushed together. Whatever it was hitting outside eventually moved. In fact, after giving a rusty creak, it moved easily as if it were rolling. When the doorway grew wide enough, they slipped through it to find themselves in the upstairs bedroom in their grandparents' house in Button Up. What had been blocking the door was Holly's bed, which now rested in the middle of the room on rollers that hadn't rolled in years. Farther down, Bridget's bed still rested snuggly against the wall.

After another minute or two of quiet, Holly said, "I'd better blow out the lantern." Stepping back through the open doorway, her voice returned in a hair-raising pitch. "Landon? Could you come here, please?"

"Yeah," said Landon numbly, gazing dreamily about the room. "Sure."

Holly had backed herself against the wall near the lantern. She was staring at the floor of the elevator. Landon glanced down. He gasped. The wood boards had been deeply scratched, as if gouged by the claw of a dragon. In fact, a tiny wisp of smoke curled up from the splintered wood. "Come on," said Landon. "Get out of there."

Holly blew out the lantern. Together they shoved the bed back against the door, which now blended almost seamlessly with the wall. "Did you know that was in there?" Landon asked. Both Bridget and Holly shook their heads. "Come on," said Landon. "Let's go find Grandpa."

Downstairs, Grandpa Karl was sitting in his leather easy chair by the dark fireplace, sipping coffee. Holly asked him about the secret room.

"Ah, yes, the hidden elevator." Grandpa Karl looked almost amused as he stroked his beard and explained. "It wasn't always hidden. I mean it's not meant to be a secret, really. We just didn't want you kids playing in it." He glanced at each of them. "For safety reasons," he added, raising his eyebrows.

"But what is it there for?" said Landon. "Why do you have an elevator?"

Grandpa Karl smiled. "We never use it, either. Here." He led them to the closet beneath the stairway. Flicking on the light, he showed them how the back wall of the closet was actually a door leading to a passageway to the elevator. The children stared.

"Creepy," said Holly.

"It goes downstairs, too," said Grandpa Karl. "It wasn't original with the house, of course. So there wasn't a perfect place to install a shaft. But your great-great-grandfather had lame legs. He couldn't climb stairs. But he wanted access to the whole house. It's been updated since then, incidentally. The original was pretty crude and unstable, operated basically like a large bucket in a well." Grandpa Karl shook his head. "Took four strong men and a pulley system to hoist the poor fellow." He chuckled.

Landon felt dazed, and he could tell Holly and Bridget were pretty much in the same boat. After thanking their grandfather for the information, the children went to Landon's bedroom—or Grandpa Karl's study—to talk.

"Did you notice?" asked Holly.

"Notice what?" replied Landon.

"He didn't ask how we got in there, how we discovered the elevator." She stared at Landon.

"Yeah," said Landon. "This house gets weirder all the time, doesn't it?"

"Did Humphrey live here, too?" Bridget piped. "Our great-great-*great*-grandfather?"

"Hmm." Landon frowned. "I've never asked. Nobody's ever

mentioned who lived here before Grandma and Grandpa."

"Landon," said Holly. He looked at her, guessing what she was thinking. "They're still there, aren't they? We're back here now, but everyone else is still on the cliff, right?" Holly's expression became pinched with concern. "And the dragon. . ."

"Volucer Ignis." It felt strange muttering his name here in the house.

"What can we do?" said Bridget. "The animals. . .and Ludo. . ."

"What's going to happen?" said Holly. "What do you think is happening there right now?"

Landon frowned. What was Volucer Ignis doing to the helpless crowd on the cliff? Had the cliff reached its full height yet? Surely it had by now. Would the people be able to fight off the dragon? Where would they go from there?

Something else bothered Landon. Well, a *lot* of things were bothering him. But something specific had been missing from their visit to the forest.

"Epops," he said suddenly, turning to his sisters. "Did anyone see Epops?" The thought of the friendly little green bird cheered him.

Holly shrugged, and then Bridget mimicked her, tilting her head. "I looked for him in the palace, you know, way up by the ceiling where some birds—"

"I think they were bats," Holly interjected. "None of them were singing or chirping." She shuddered.

"Were flying around," Bridget continued. "But I didn't see him. I don't think he was there. He would have come down to say, 'Hi.' " She nodded confidently.

"Hmm," said Landon. "Maybe we just missed him. Or he missed us. I hope he's all right."

They sat quietly. "Maybe we should pray," Landon said. "I'm not sure what else we can do from here." The girls nodded. Before closing his eyes, however, Landon asked them, "If we could go back, even right now, to help and fight, would we want to? Do you want to?"

Holly blinked, and Bridget sighed. "Those were some sharp claws," Holly said thoughtfully.

"He's a meanie," said Bridget firmly. "I hate that dragon. And Max. And the Arcans."

Landon nodded, glancing down. He was rubbing his fingers together where the blueberry seed had been. Suddenly, his sisters both declared, "Yes. I'll go." And then they smiled at one another and laughed.

"Me, too," said Landon. "So we're all in. Now we just need to figure out how to get back quickly and hope we're not too late."

Something was moving on the desk. His Bible! The pages were turning, flipping rapidly from one side to the other. Landon stood, and his sisters followed. They watched in awe as the final page settled. Landon leaned close. Underlined were these words in Joshua 10:13:

> *And the sun stood still, and the moon stayed, until the people had avenged themselves upon their enemies. . . . So the sun stood still in the midst of heaven, and hasted not to go down about a whole day.*

Landon looked up, staring at nothing. Cogs in his brain began turning.

"Are you thinking what I'm thinking?" Holly asked him after she'd read the verse aloud. "Do you think—"

"Nothing is happening there right now," said Landon. His thoughts and his voice seemed far off. Gradually his focus returned to the study. "It's like they're frozen in time. 'The sun stood still. . . .' "

"So," said Holly glancing at the clock, "we have about twenty-four hours to get back there and save the day." She sounded a little excited.

Bridget chimed in. "Um—when are Mom and Dad coming to pick us up?"

Landon looked at the clock. Their parents were due to arrive. . . .

"In about eight or nine hours," he said.

The girls inhaled deeply. "Well," said Holly, "where do we start?"

"With prayer," said Bridget. "Remember?"

Landon looked at her and smiled. "Good idea, Bridge. Let's do that."

The children prayed together, seeking help and guidance and strength and courage and wisdom. After a resounding "Amen," Holly and Bridget left the room to get something to eat. Landon paused by the desk and noticed the Bible had turned more pages while they were praying. He read the words underlined in Matthew 17:20:

> *If ye have faith as a grain of mustard seed, ye shall say unto this mountain, Remove hence to yonder place; and it shall remove; and nothing shall be impossible unto you.*

Landon smiled. "Or a blueberry seed," he said. "Speaking of which. . ."

He patted his growling stomach and went to the kitchen.

After breakfast, the girls went upstairs to bed. They were all exhausted and needed at least a couple hours of rest. Neither Holly nor Bridget seemed to appreciate Landon's joke that they take the elevator.

Tired as he was, something compelled Landon to go outside. The morning light glowed faintly. The fresh air tasted good. He heard a noise. Rounding the corner of the house to investigate, Landon was surprised to see Grandpa Karl walking from the barn toward the house.

Landon waited for his grandfather to enter the house through the back door. Moving briskly from the house to the barn, Landon checked the side door: locked. The large barn door, however, which had been converted years ago into a vertically sliding garage door, was unlocked. Before raising it, Landon noticed sawdust and a couple curled wood shavings on the ground.

That's strange, he thought. He didn't know Grandpa Karl did any woodworking; he only came out here to work on his jalopy.

The door creaked and groaned, and Landon held his breath. Inside it smelled of oil and grease, and indeed there was the old car that Landon had never seen run.

More sawdust and a wood chip caught Landon's eye, leading him to the rear of the garage. Another door waited, and Landon's heart rate climbed as he approached. On the floor in front of the door was a single black blot. Landon stooped for a closer look.

Oddly, it appeared fresh—*still damp*—and was too dark to be oil. Landon touched it, drawing back a blackened fingertip. It looked like paint, or thick, dark lacquer.

The door was unlocked.

Landon stepped into a dark space. He could tell the room was large and open. It smelled of wood and paint. Searching along the wall to his right, he found a switch.

He flipped it on, illuminating the room.

Before him loomed a towering figure—some sort of statue, it seemed—covered with a vast canvas tarp. The tarp drooped slightly at the top between two points. Scaffolding stood along one side, rising over two stories high.

As Landon walked into the room, he nearly bumped into a sawhorse. A plank rested across it and another sawhorse. In the middle of the plank stood a single chess piece: a dark knight. Landon picked it up and held it at eye level.

"What are *you* doing here?" he said.

Landon remembered being on a huge chessboard when a giant dark knight approached him. The knight had been about two stories tall.

Landon's stomach did a somersault.

Closing one eye, Landon matched the knight's ears with the statue's twin points beneath the tarp. When he lowered the knights, Landon noticed hinges in the floor running on either side of the statue. It looked like a big trapdoor right below the statue.

Landon hastily set the knight on the plank, his hand trembling. Landon left the barn and returned to the house, puzzling over the giant statue and the big trapdoor. When he reached the house he stopped and looked back. Had he just discovered another way back to Wonderwood?

About the Author

R. K. Mortenson, an ordained minister in the Church of the Lutheran Brethren, has been writing poems and stories since he was a kid. *Landon Snow and the Volucer Dragon* is his fourth novel. A former Navy chaplain, Mortenson is a pastor in North Dakota. He serves a church in Mayville, where he lives with his wife, daughter, and two sons.

Other books by R. K. Mortenson:

Landon Snow
and the Auctor's Riddle

Landon Snow
and the Shadows of Malus Quidam

Landon Snow
and the Island of Arcanum